# GOTTA CATCH A *WHAT*?!

## 2 GRAPHIC ADVENTURES

Adapted by
Simcha Whitehill

*graphix*

An Imprint of
**SCHOLASTIC**

©2022 Pokémon. ©1997–2019 Nintendo, Creatures, GAME FREAK, TV Tokyo, ShoPro, JR Kikaku. TM, ® Nintendo.

All rights reserved. Published by Graphix, an imprint of Scholastic Inc., *Publishers since 1920.* SCHOLASTIC, GRAPHIX, and associated logos are trademarks and/or registered trademarks of Scholastic Inc.

The publisher does not have any control over and does not assume any responsibility for author or third-party websites or their content.

No part of this publication may be reproduced, stored in a retrieval system, or transmitted in any form or by any means, electronic, mechanical, photocopying, recording, or otherwise, without written permission of the publisher. For information regarding permission, write to Scholastic Inc., Attention: Permissions Department, 557 Broadway, New York, NY 10012.

This book is a work of fiction. Names, characters, places, and incidents are either the product of the author's imagination or are used fictitiously, and any resemblance to actual persons, living or dead, business establishments, events, or locales is entirely coincidental.

ISBN 978-1-338-81994-6 (paperback)
ISBN 978-1-338-81995-3 (hardcover)

10 9 8 7 6 5 4 3 2 1          22 23 24 25 26

Designed by Cheung Tai

Printed in China                    62
First printing 2022

# CONTENTS

# Story 1: A Far-Fetched Battle

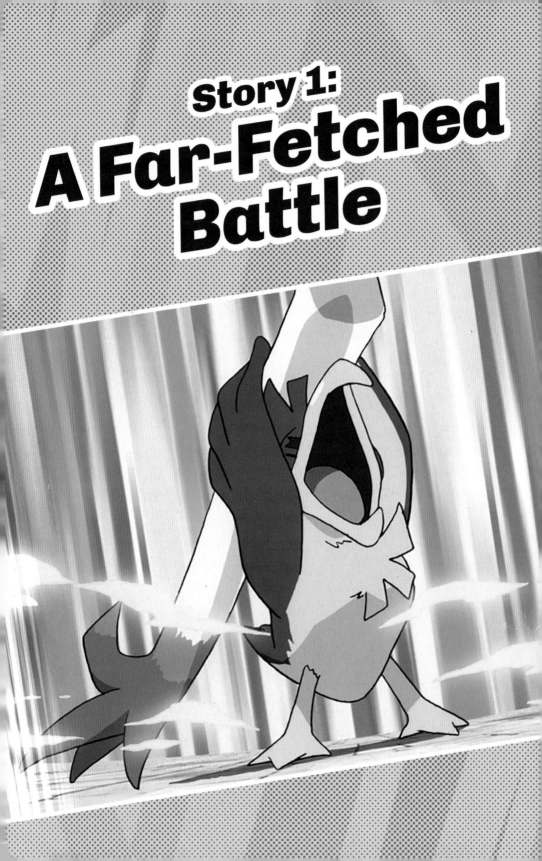

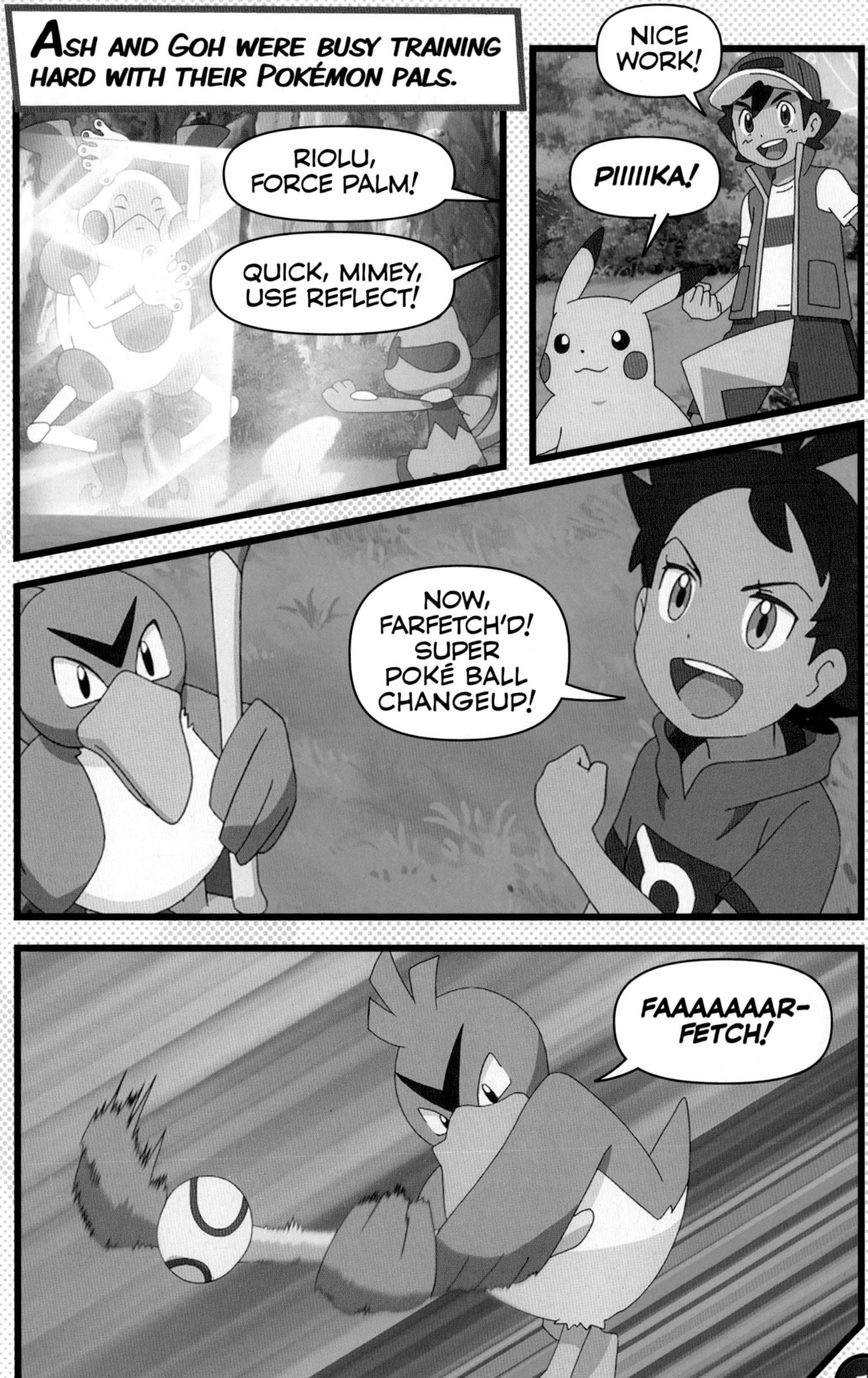
ASH AND GOH WERE BUSY TRAINING HARD WITH THEIR POKÉMON PALS.
RIOLU, FORCE PALM!
QUICK, MIMEY, USE REFLECT!
NICE WORK!
PIIIIKA!
NOW, FARFETCH'D! SUPER POKÉ BALL CHANGEUP!
FAAAAAAAR-FETCH!

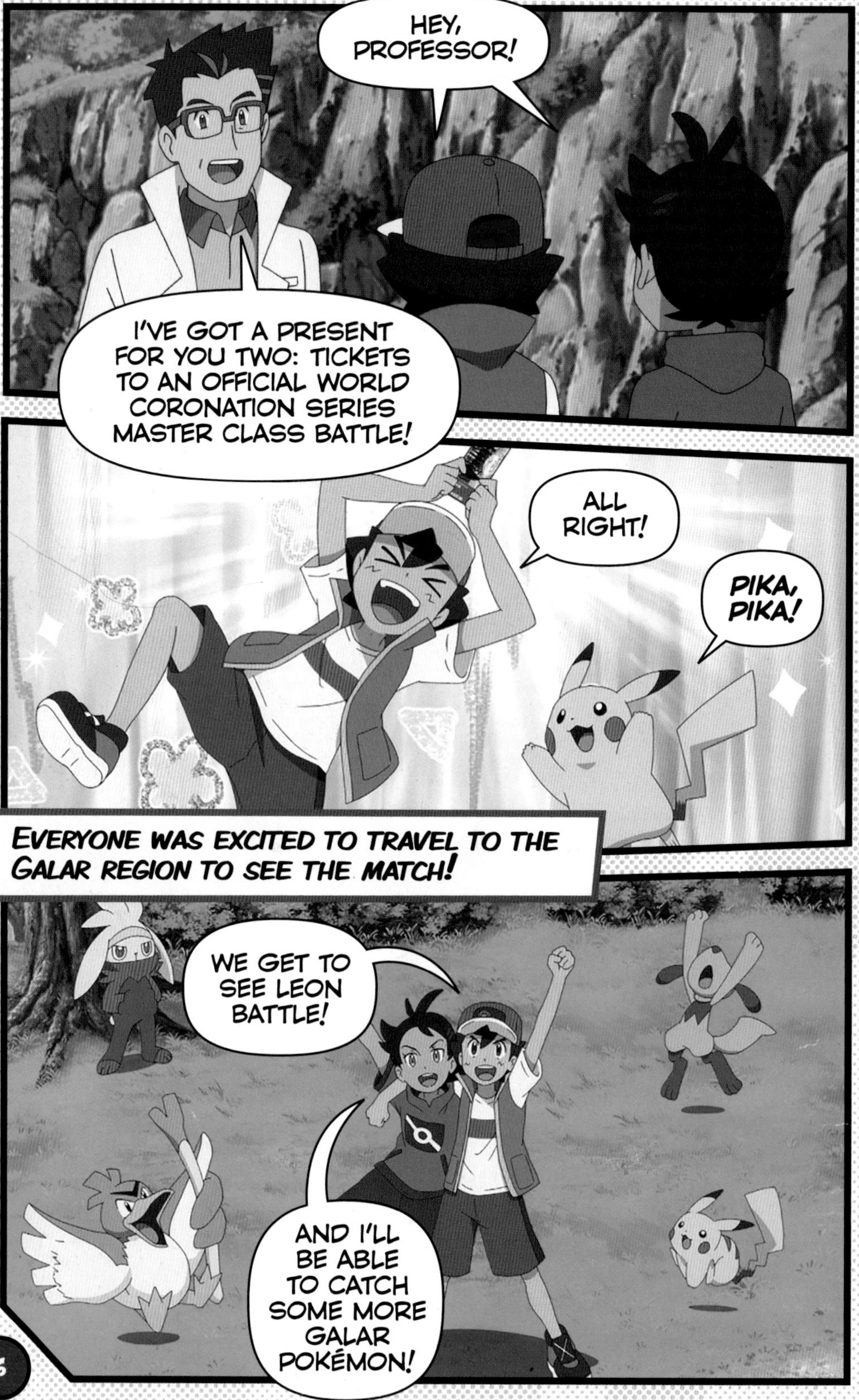
HEY, PROFESSOR!
I'VE GOT A PRESENT FOR YOU TWO: TICKETS TO AN OFFICIAL WORLD CORONATION SERIES MASTER CLASS BATTLE!
ALL RIGHT!
PIKA, PIKA!
EVERYONE WAS EXCITED TO TRAVEL TO THE GALAR REGION TO SEE THE MATCH!
WE GET TO SEE LEON BATTLE!
AND I'LL BE ABLE TO CATCH SOME MORE GALAR POKÉMON!

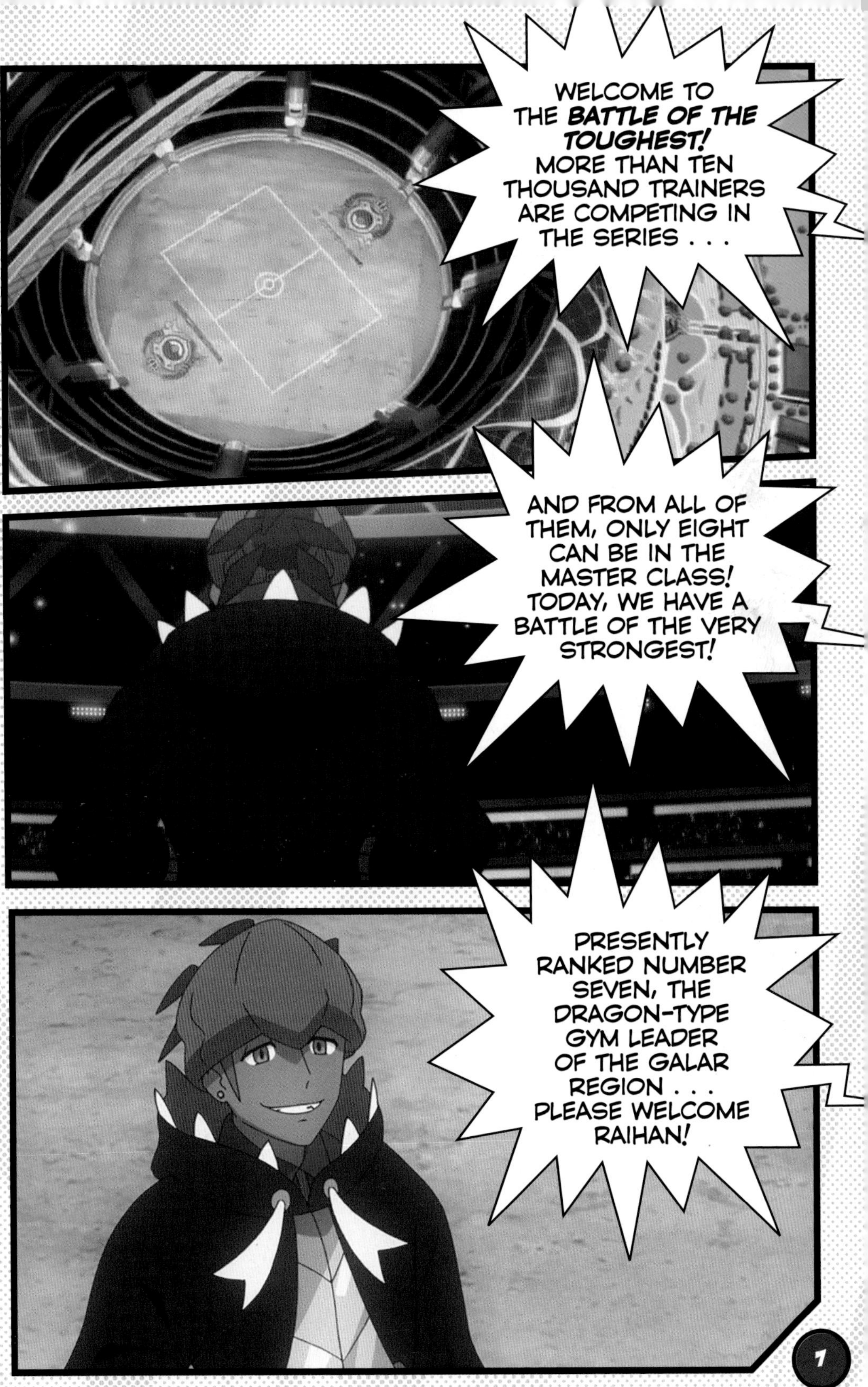

WELCOME TO THE ***BATTLE OF THE TOUGHEST!*** MORE THAN TEN THOUSAND TRAINERS ARE COMPETING IN THE SERIES . . .
AND FROM ALL OF THEM, ONLY EIGHT CAN BE IN THE MASTER CLASS! TODAY, WE HAVE A BATTLE OF THE VERY STRONGEST!
PRESENTLY RANKED NUMBER SEVEN, THE DRAGON-TYPE GYM LEADER OF THE GALAR REGION . . . PLEASE WELCOME RAIHAN!

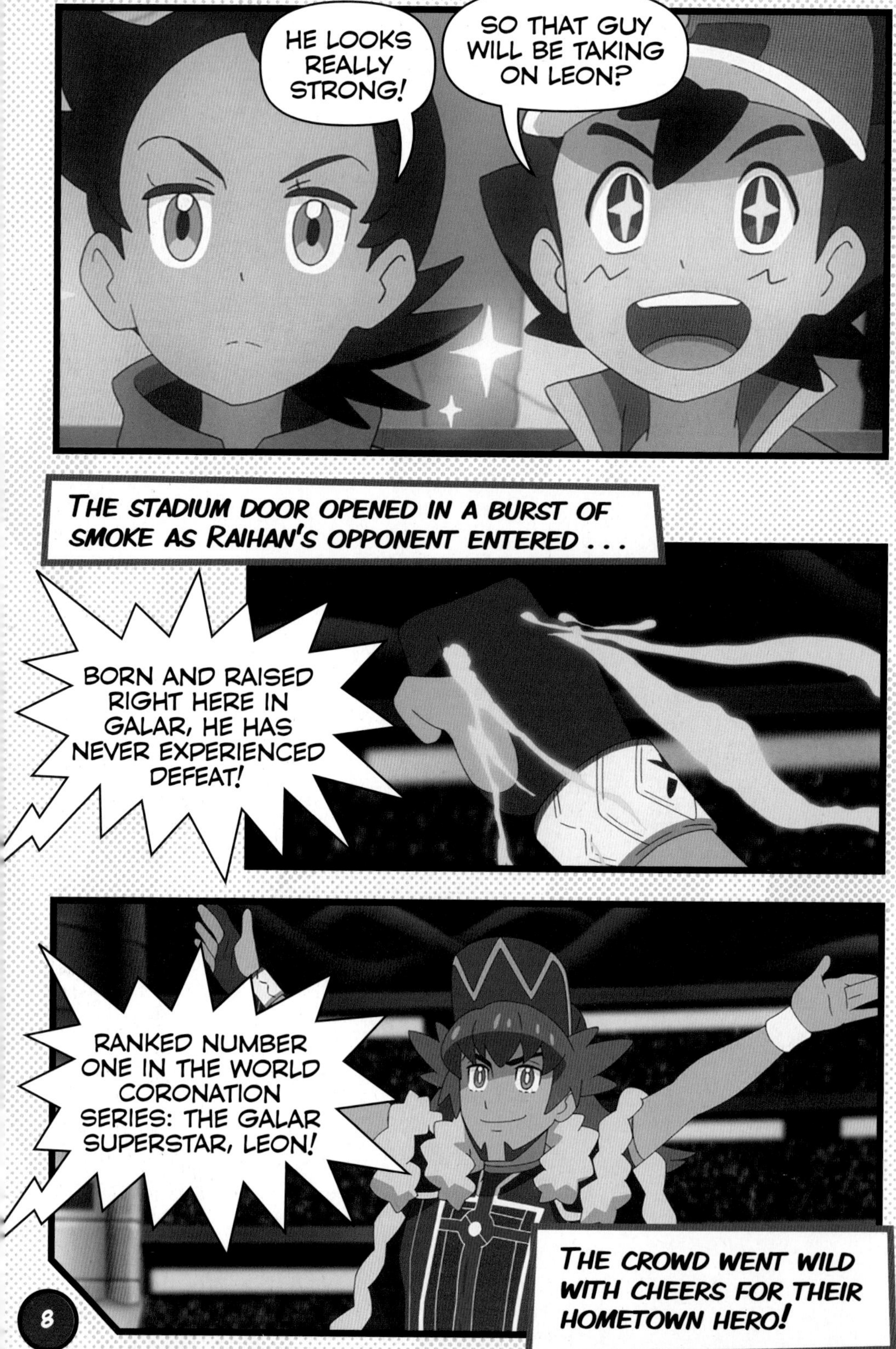
HE LOOKS REALLY STRONG!
SO THAT GUY WILL BE TAKING ON LEON?
THE STADIUM DOOR OPENED IN A BURST OF SMOKE AS RAIHAN'S OPPONENT ENTERED . . .
BORN AND RAISED RIGHT HERE IN GALAR, HE HAS NEVER EXPERIENCED DEFEAT!
RANKED NUMBER ONE IN THE WORLD CORONATION SERIES: THE GALAR SUPERSTAR, LEON!
THE CROWD WENT WILD WITH CHEERS FOR THEIR HOMETOWN HERO!

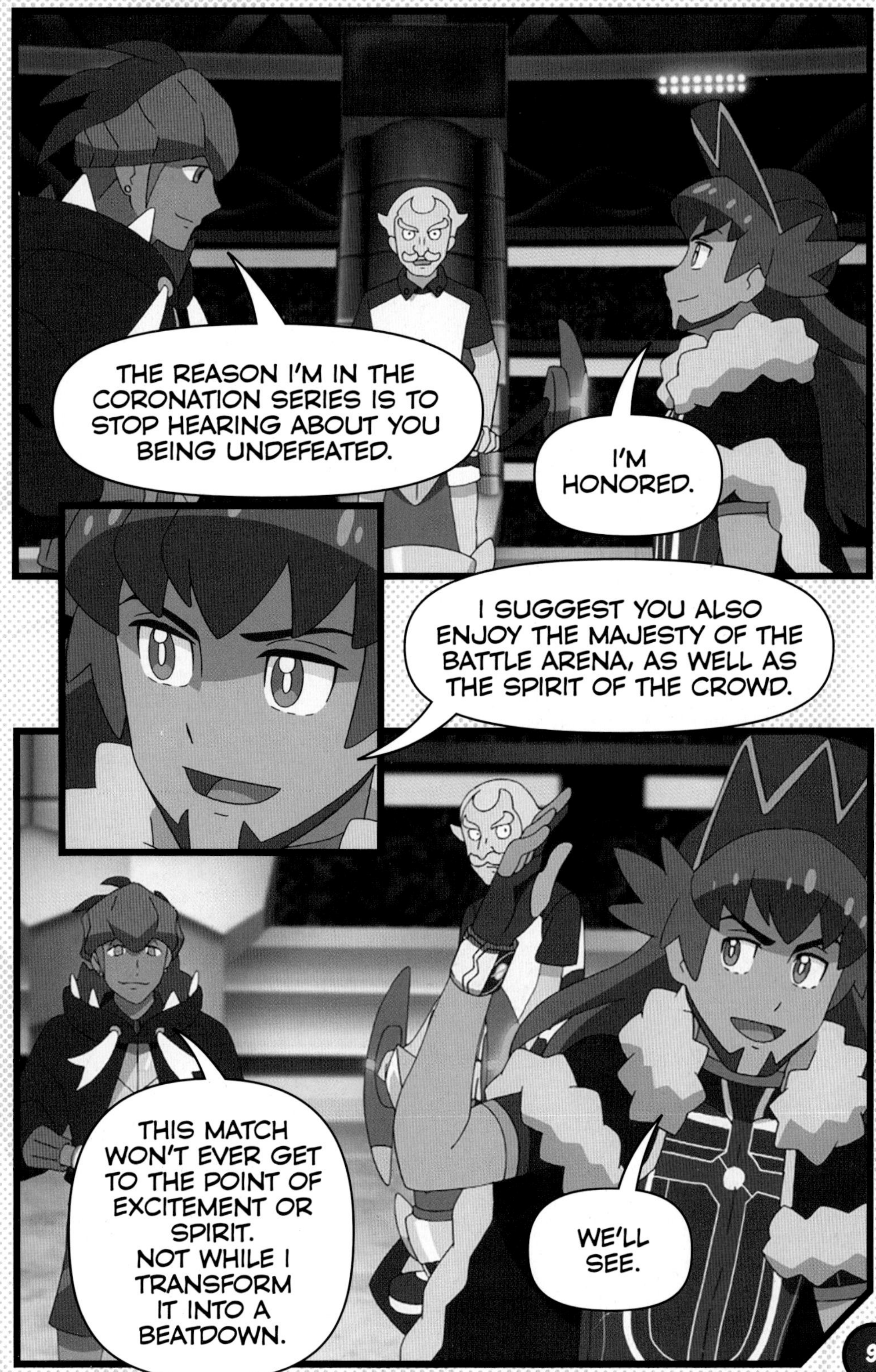
THE REASON I'M IN THE CORONATION SERIES IS TO STOP HEARING ABOUT YOU BEING UNDEFEATED.
I'M HONORED.
I SUGGEST YOU ALSO ENJOY THE MAJESTY OF THE BATTLE ARENA, AS WELL AS THE SPIRIT OF THE CROWD.
THIS MATCH WON'T EVER GET TO THE POINT OF EXCITEMENT OR SPIRIT. NOT WHILE I TRANSFORM IT INTO A BEATDOWN.
WE'LL SEE.

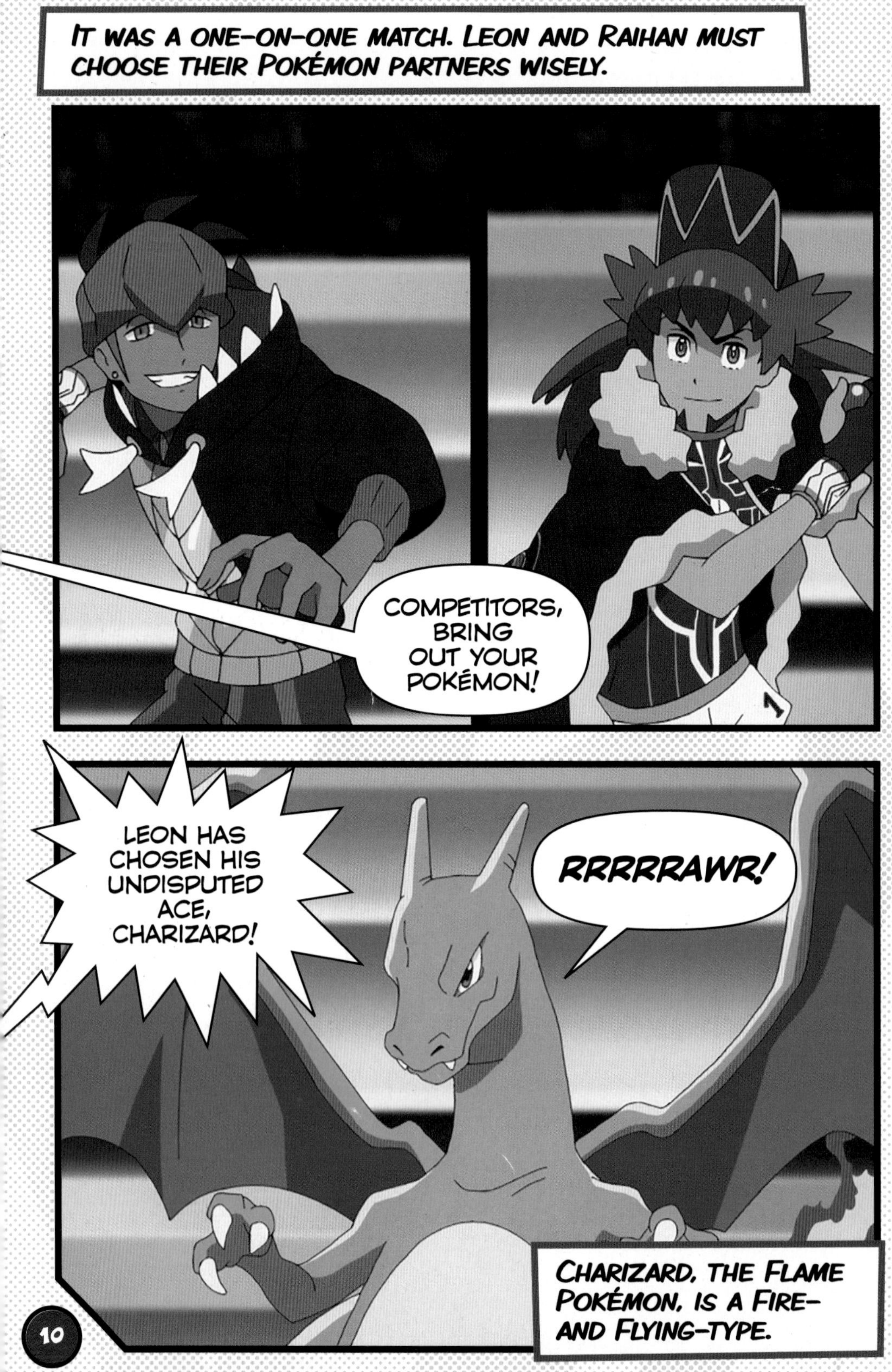
IT WAS A ONE-ON-ONE MATCH. LEON AND RAIHAN MUST CHOOSE THEIR POKÉMON PARTNERS WISELY.
COMPETITORS, BRING OUT YOUR POKÉMON!
LEON HAS CHOSEN HIS UNDISPUTED ACE, CHARIZARD!
RRRRRAWR!
CHARIZARD, THE FLAME POKÉMON, IS A FIRE- AND FLYING-TYPE.

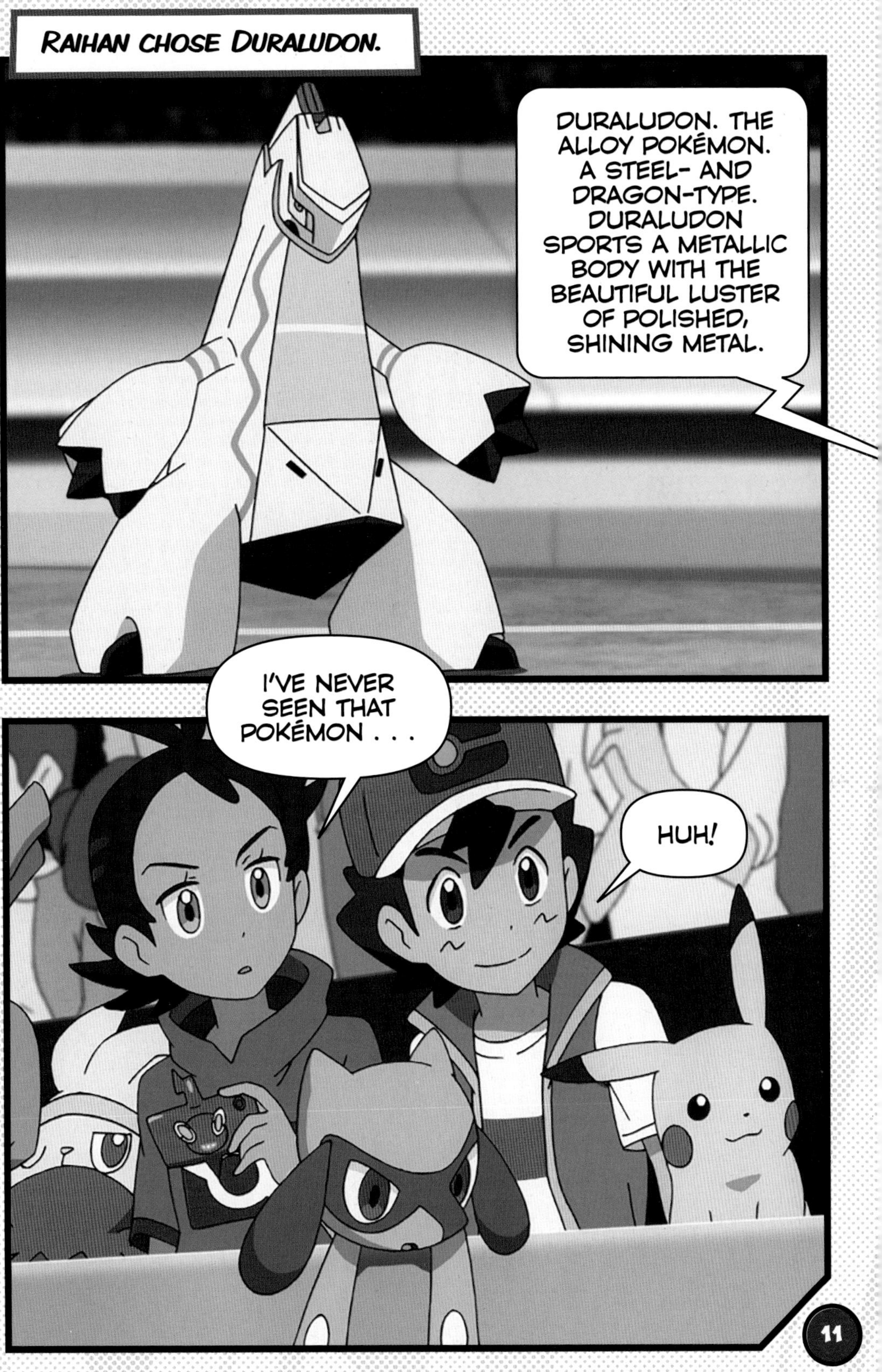
RAIHAN CHOSE DURALUDON.
DURALUDON. THE ALLOY POKÉMON. A STEEL- AND DRAGON-TYPE. DURALUDON SPORTS A METALLIC BODY WITH THE BEAUTIFUL LUSTER OF POLISHED, SHINING METAL.
I'VE NEVER SEEN THAT POKÉMON . . .
HUH!

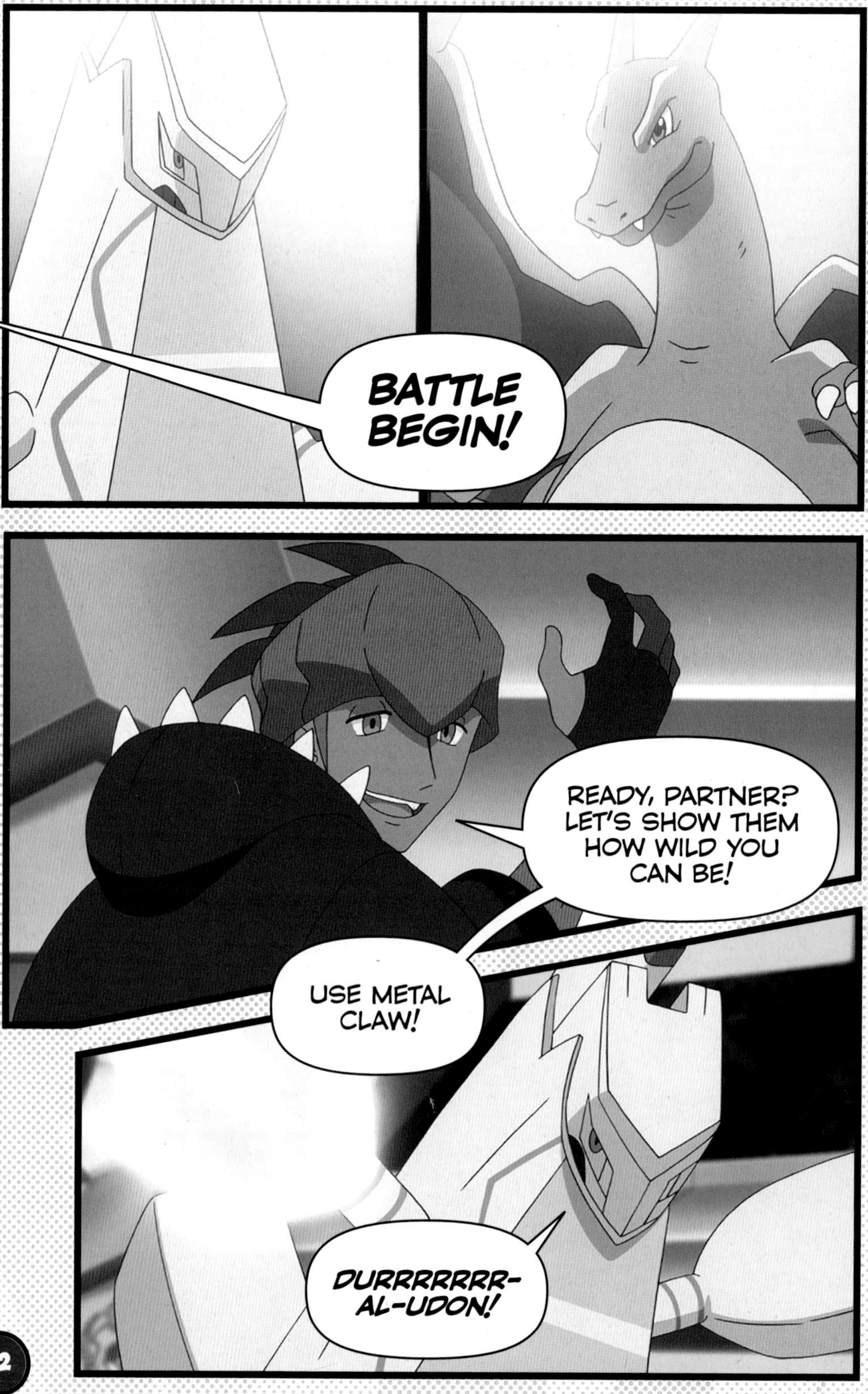
BATTLE BEGIN!
READY, PARTNER? LET'S SHOW THEM HOW WILD YOU CAN BE!
USE METAL CLAW!
DURRRRRRR-AL-UDON!

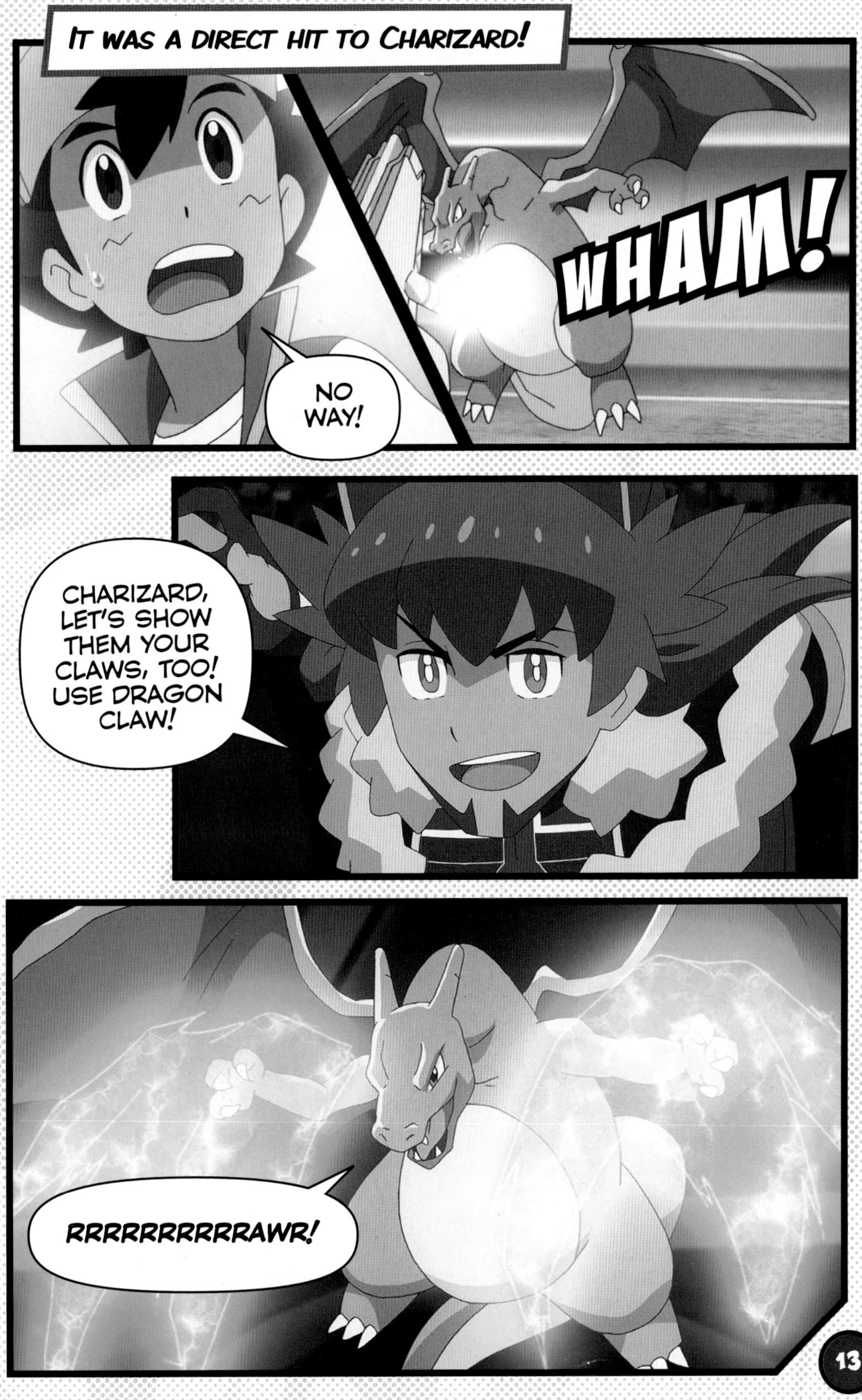
It was a direct hit to Charizard!
WHAM!
NO WAY!
CHARIZARD, LET'S SHOW THEM YOUR CLAWS, TOO! USE DRAGON CLAW!
RRRRRRRRRRAWR!

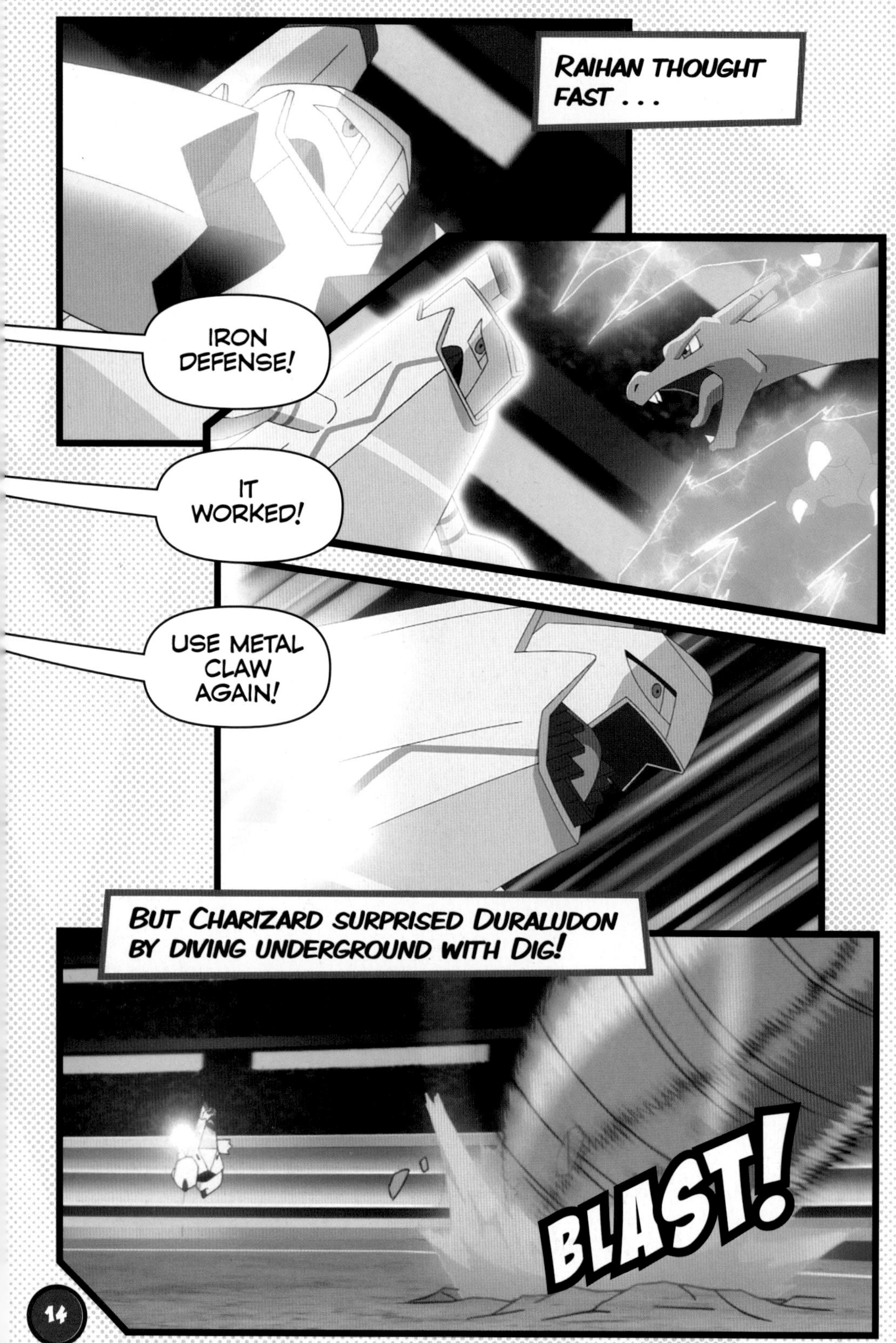
RAIHAN THOUGHT FAST . . .
IRON DEFENSE!
IT WORKED!
USE METAL CLAW AGAIN!
BUT CHARIZARD SURPRISED DURALUDON BY DIVING UNDERGROUND WITH DIG!
BLAST!

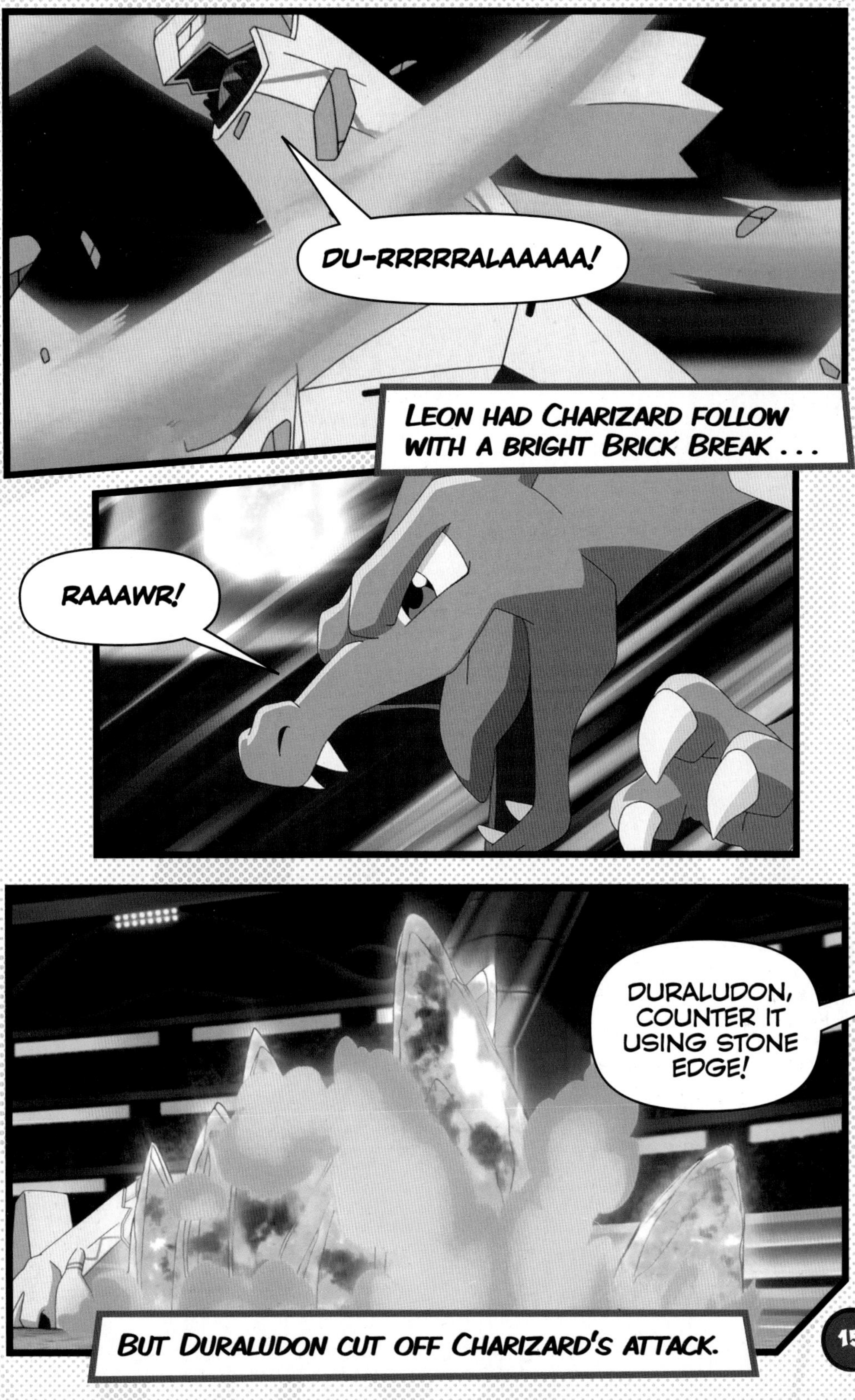
DU-RRRRRALAAAAA!
LEON HAD CHARIZARD FOLLOW WITH A BRIGHT BRICK BREAK . . .
RAAAWR!
DURALUDON, COUNTER IT USING STONE EDGE!
BUT DURALUDON CUT OFF CHARIZARD'S ATTACK.

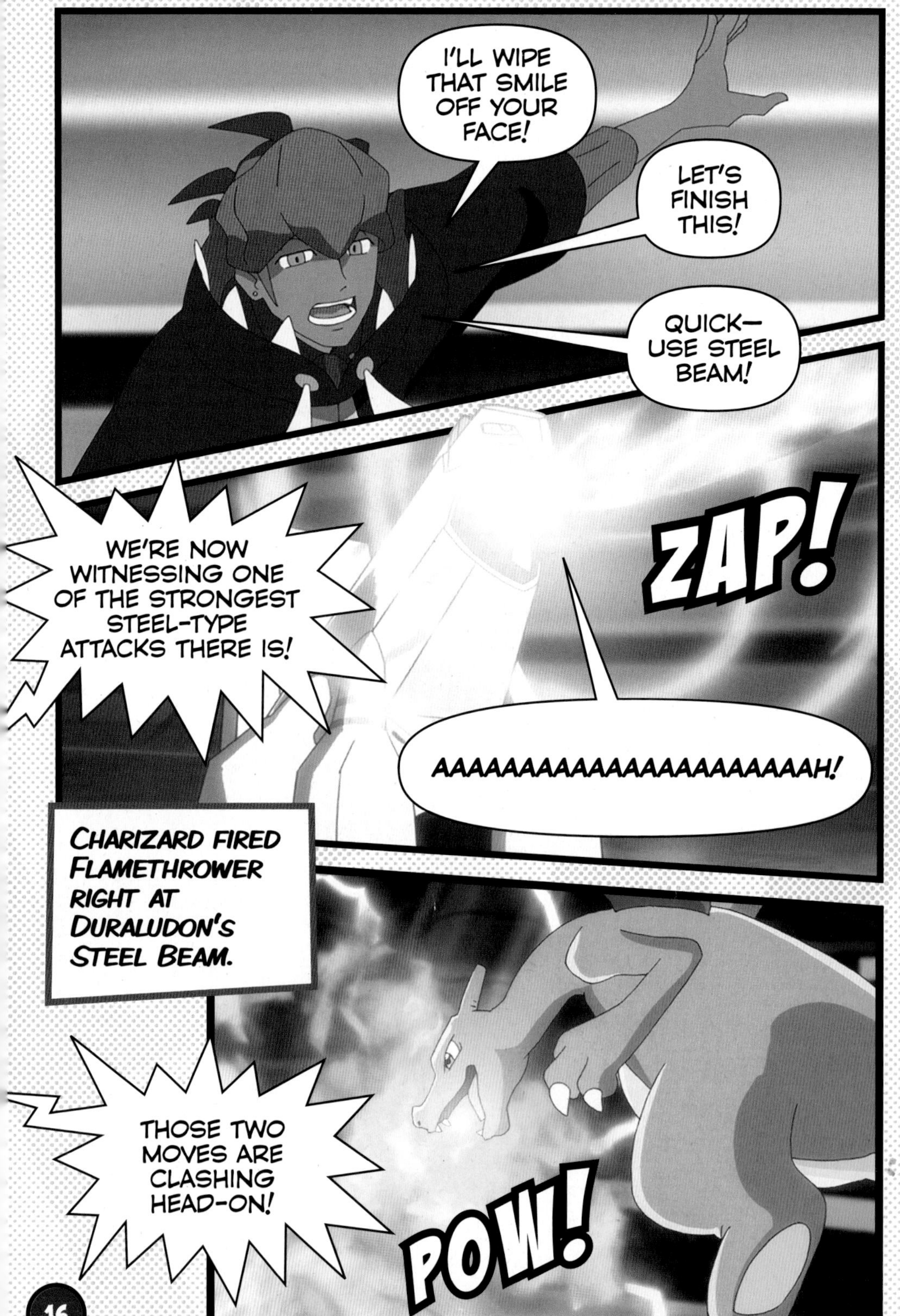
I'LL WIPE THAT SMILE OFF YOUR FACE!
LET'S FINISH THIS!
QUICK—USE STEEL BEAM!
WE'RE NOW WITNESSING ONE OF THE STRONGEST STEEL-TYPE ATTACKS THERE IS!
ZAP!
AAAAAAAAAAAAAAAAAAAAAAAH!
CHARIZARD FIRED FLAMETHROWER RIGHT AT DURALUDON'S STEEL BEAM.
THOSE TWO MOVES ARE CLASHING HEAD-ON!
POW!

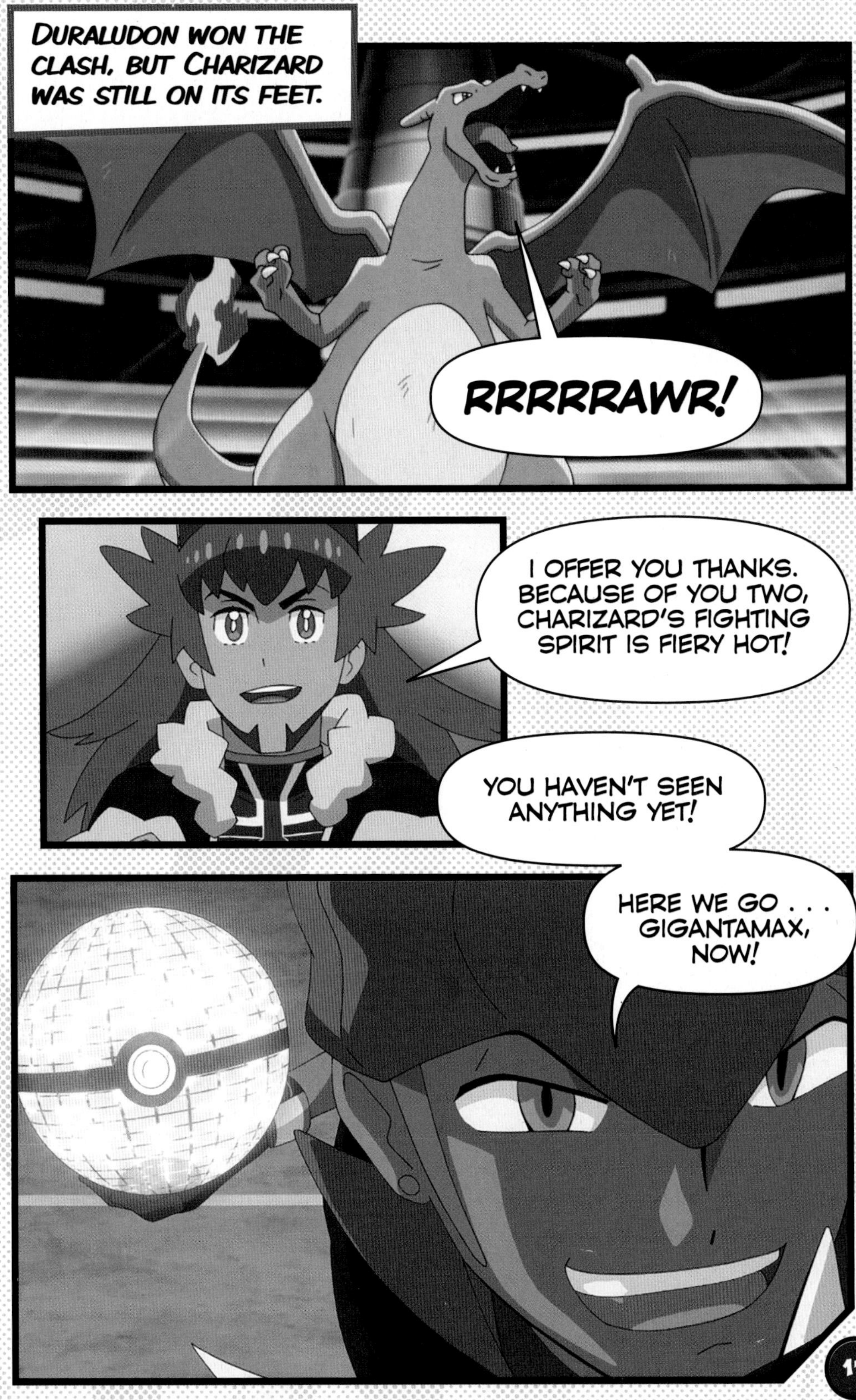
DURALUDON WON THE CLASH, BUT CHARIZARD WAS STILL ON ITS FEET.
RRRRRAWR!
I OFFER YOU THANKS. BECAUSE OF YOU TWO, CHARIZARD'S FIGHTING SPIRIT IS FIERY HOT!
YOU HAVEN'T SEEN ANYTHING YET!
HERE WE GO . . . GIGANTAMAX, NOW!

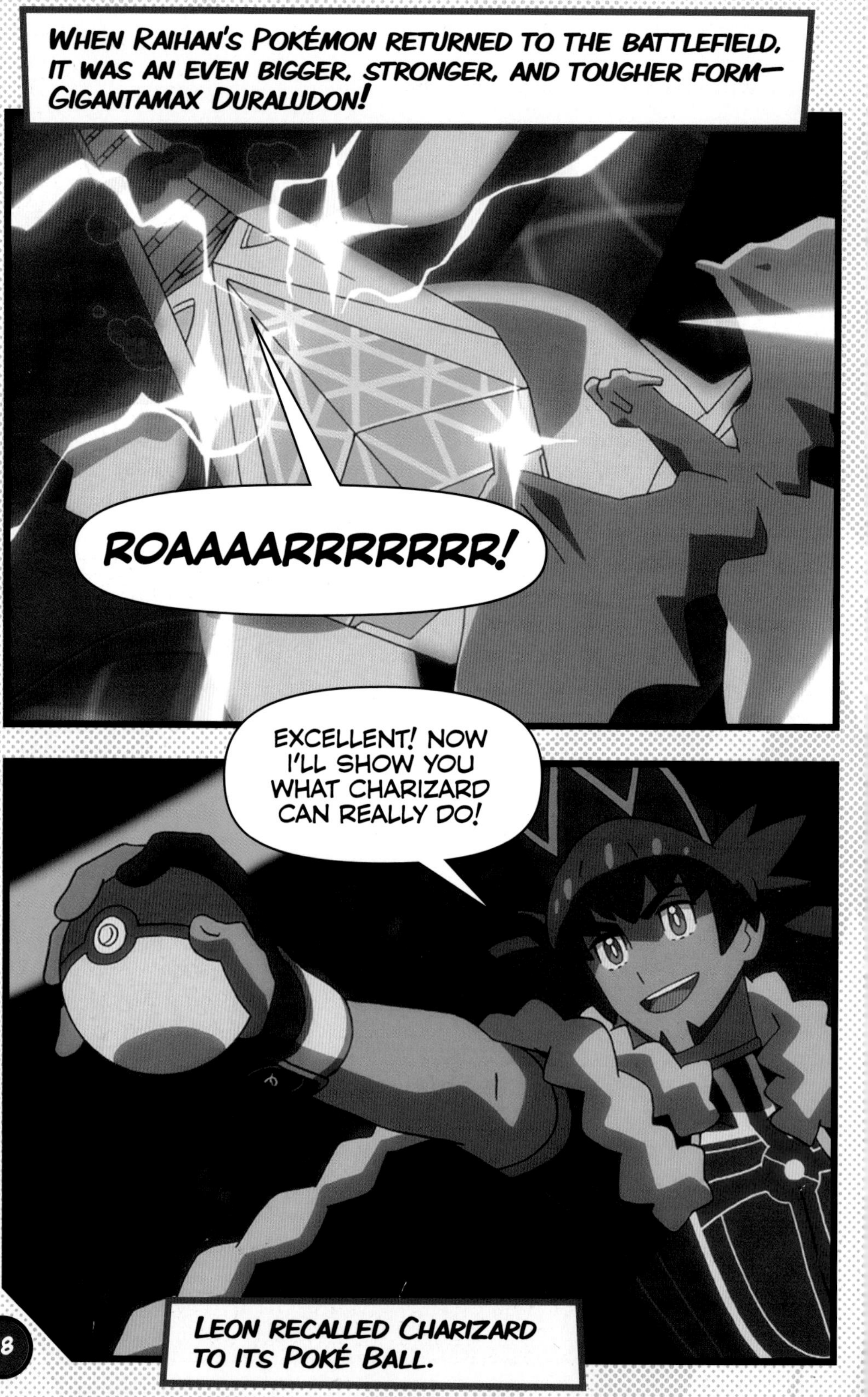
WHEN RAIHAN'S POKÉMON RETURNED TO THE BATTLEFIELD, IT WAS AN EVEN BIGGER, STRONGER, AND TOUGHER FORM—GIGANTAMAX DURALUDON!
ROAAAARRRRRRR!
EXCELLENT! NOW I'LL SHOW YOU WHAT CHARIZARD CAN REALLY DO!
LEON RECALLED CHARIZARD TO ITS POKÉ BALL.

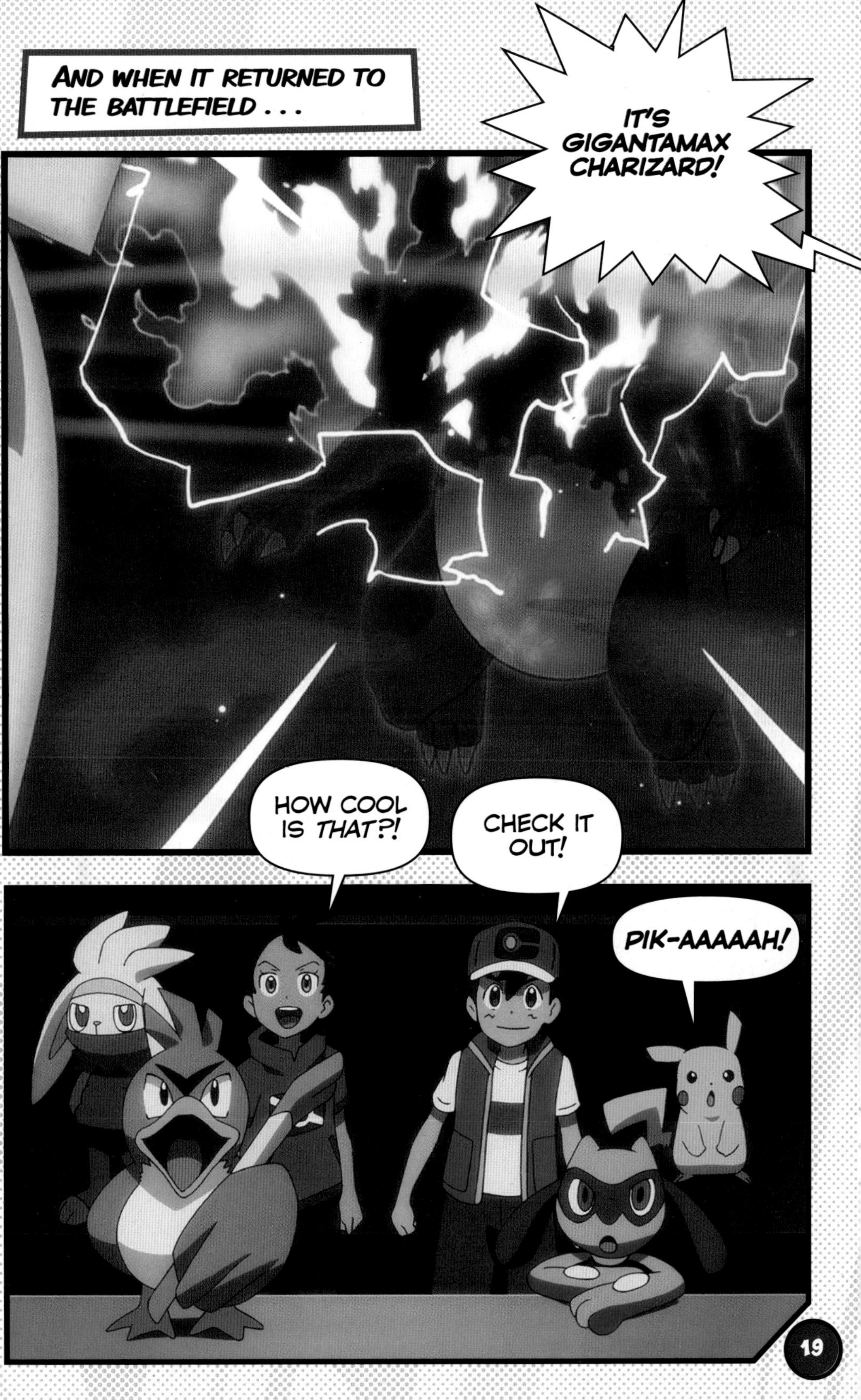
AND WHEN IT RETURNED TO THE BATTLEFIELD . . .
IT'S GIGANTAMAX CHARIZARD!
HOW COOL IS *THAT*?!
CHECK IT OUT!
PIK-AAAAAH!

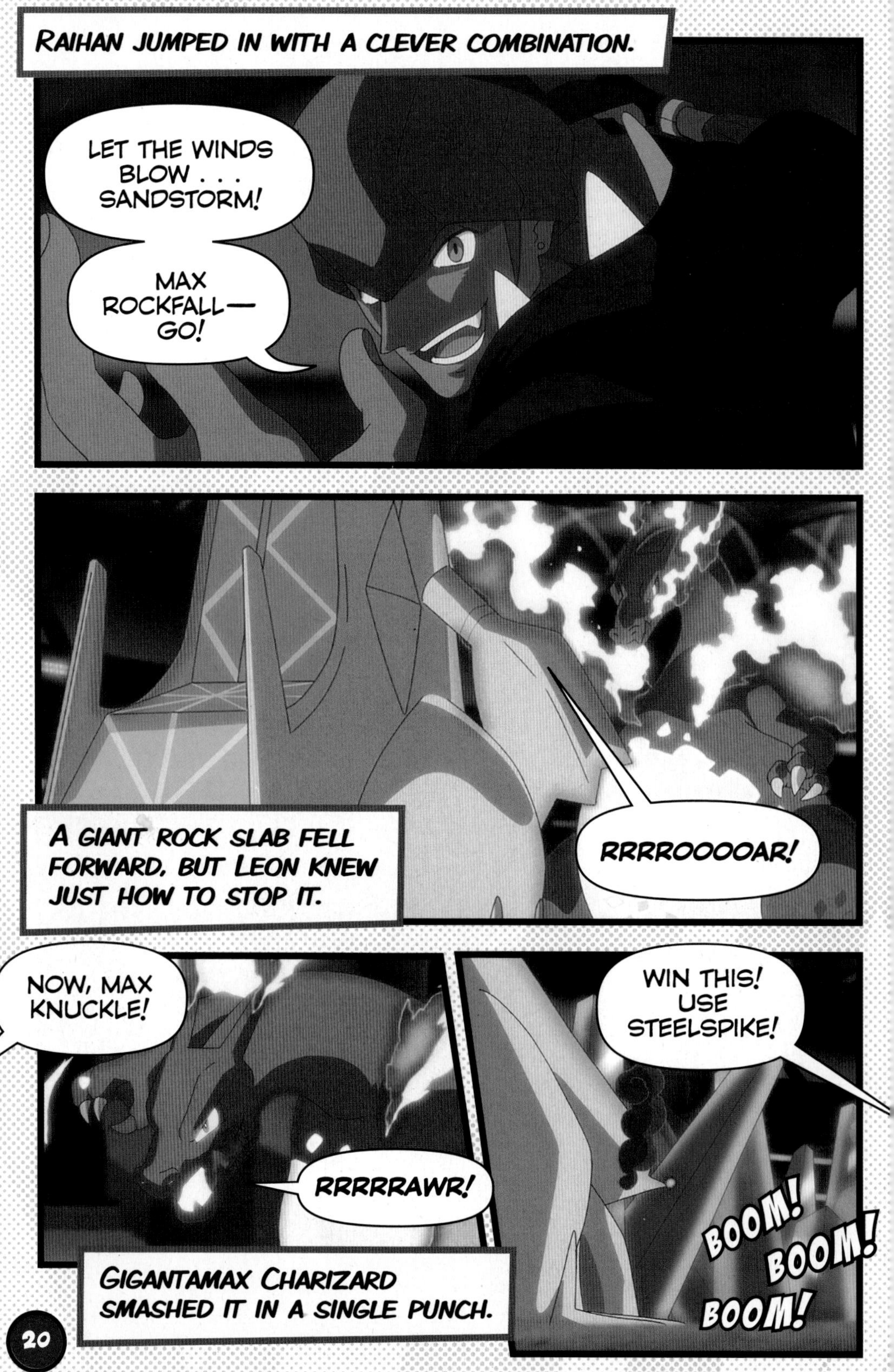
RAIHAN JUMPED IN WITH A CLEVER COMBINATION.
LET THE WINDS BLOW . . . SANDSTORM!
MAX ROCKFALL—GO!
A GIANT ROCK SLAB FELL FORWARD, BUT LEON KNEW JUST HOW TO STOP IT.
RRRROOOOAR!
NOW, MAX KNUCKLE!
RRRRRAWR!
GIGANTAMAX CHARIZARD SMASHED IT IN A SINGLE PUNCH.
WIN THIS! USE STEELSPIKE!
BOOM! BOOM! BOOM!

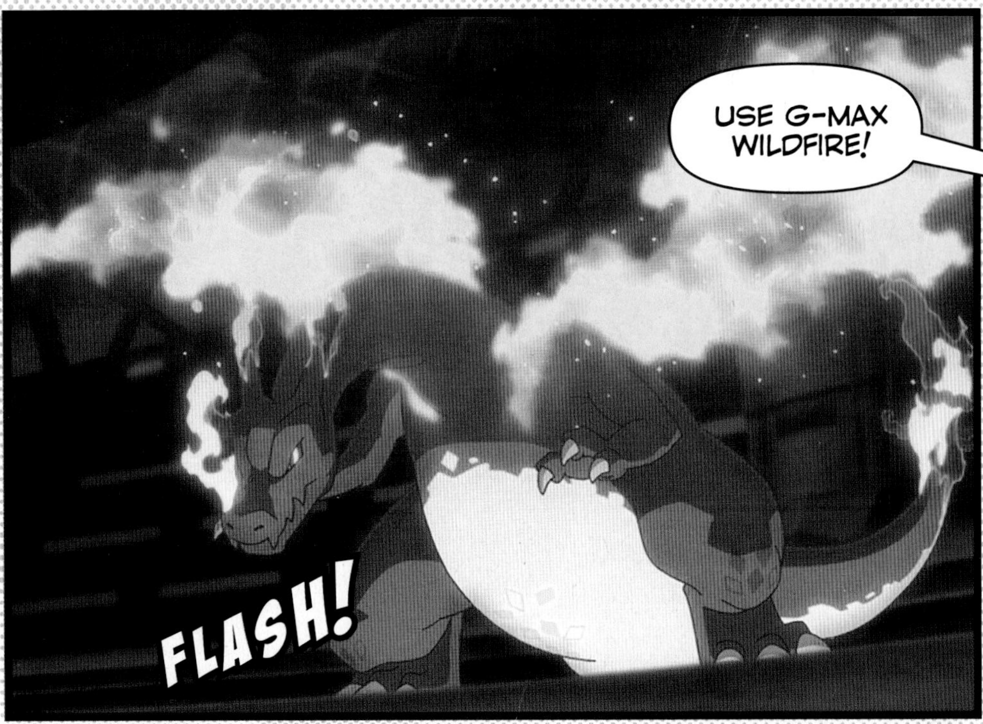
USE G-MAX WILDFIRE!
FLASH!

*GIGANTAMAX CHARIZARD'S WILDFIRE SLICED RIGHT THROUGH STEELSPIKE.*

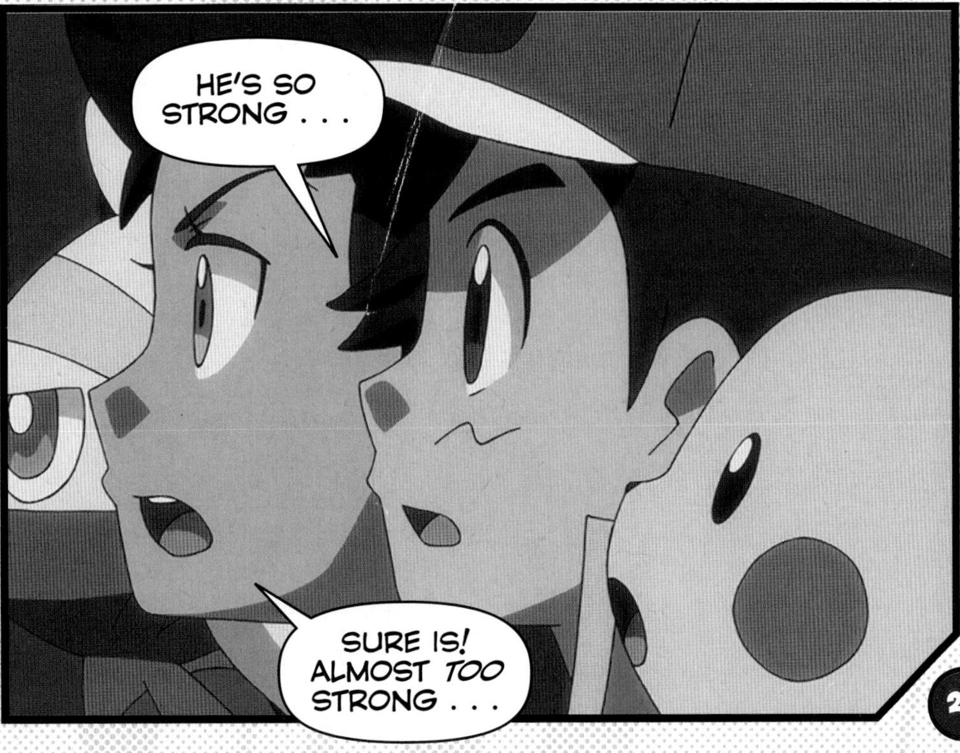
HE'S SO STRONG . . .
SURE IS! ALMOST *TOO* STRONG . . .

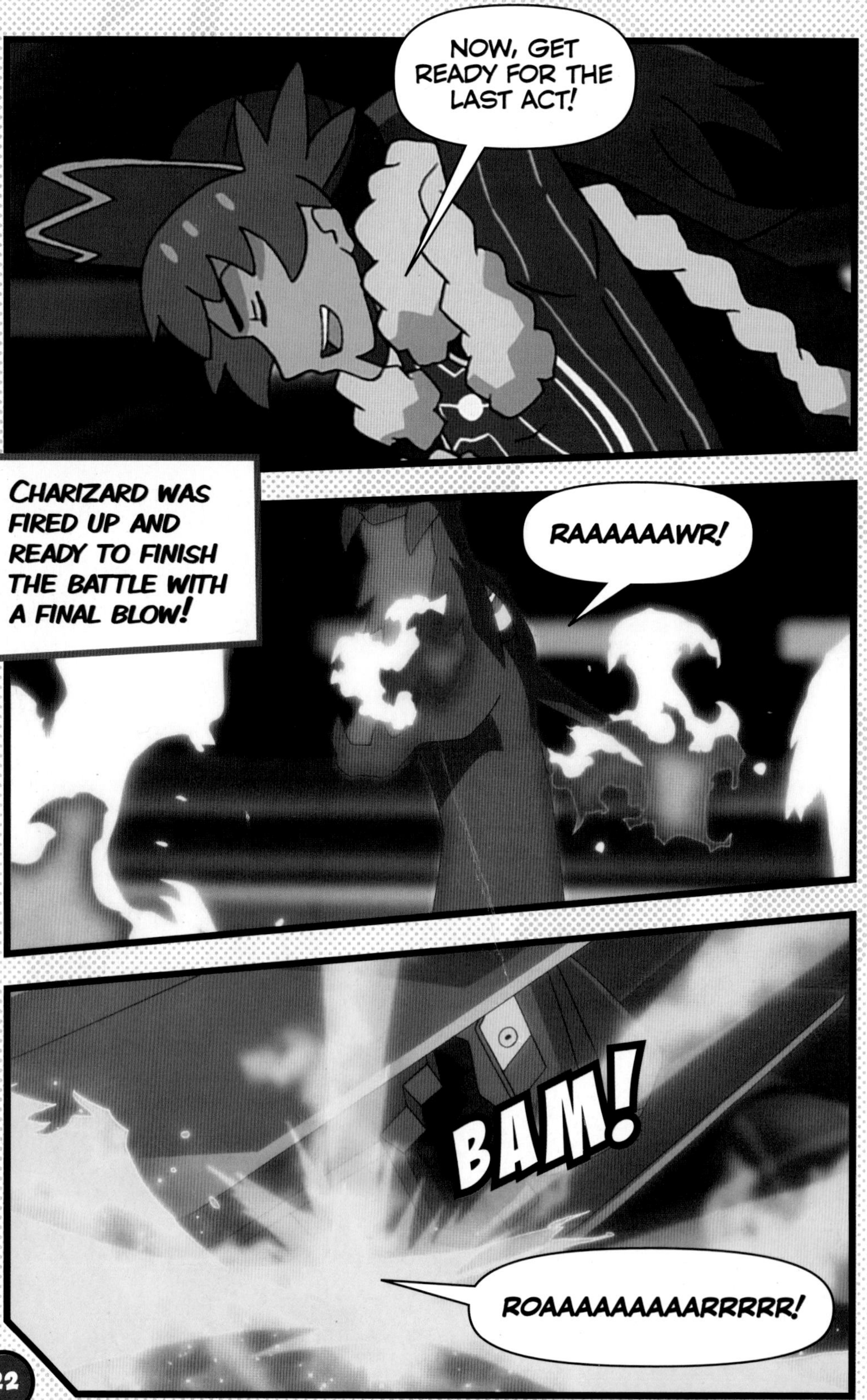
NOW, GET READY FOR THE LAST ACT!
CHARIZARD WAS FIRED UP AND READY TO FINISH THE BATTLE WITH A FINAL BLOW!
RAAAAAAAWR!
BAM!
ROAAAAAAAAARRRRR!

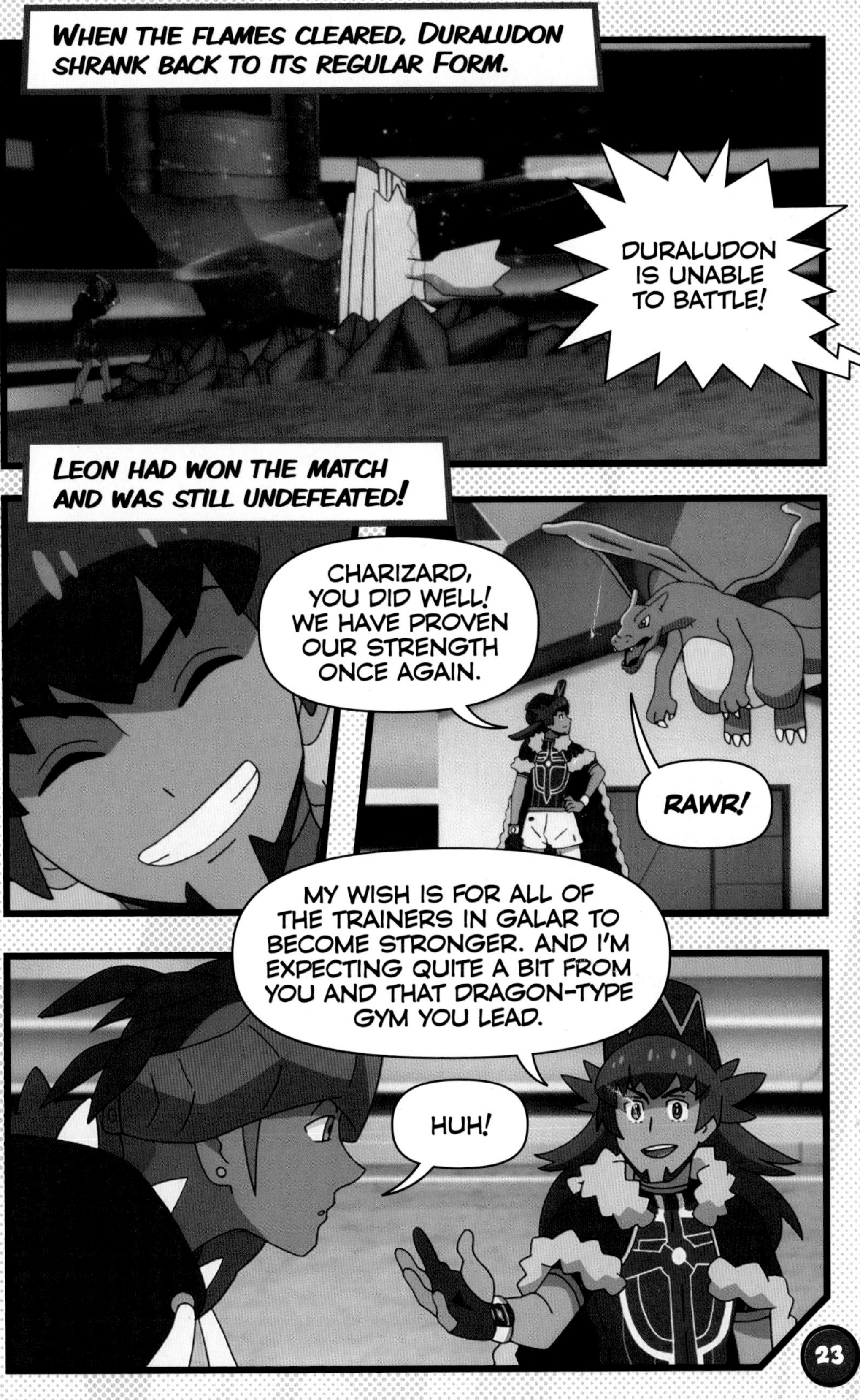
WHEN THE FLAMES CLEARED, DURALUDON SHRANK BACK TO ITS REGULAR FORM.
DURALUDON IS UNABLE TO BATTLE!
LEON HAD WON THE MATCH AND WAS STILL UNDEFEATED!
CHARIZARD, YOU DID WELL! WE HAVE PROVEN OUR STRENGTH ONCE AGAIN.
RAWR!
MY WISH IS FOR ALL OF THE TRAINERS IN GALAR TO BECOME STRONGER. AND I'M EXPECTING QUITE A BIT FROM YOU AND THAT DRAGON-TYPE GYM YOU LEAD.
HUH!

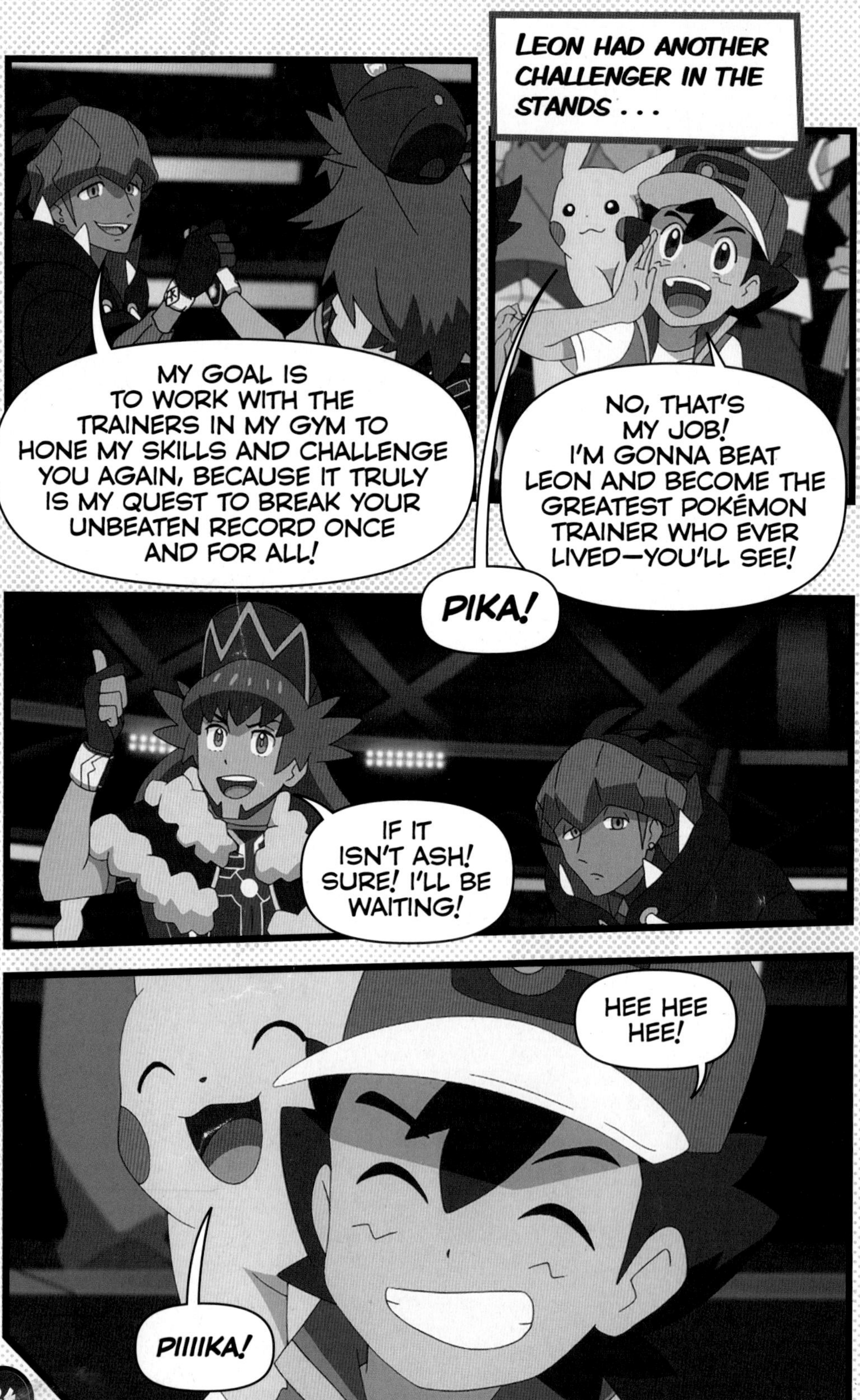
MY GOAL IS TO WORK WITH THE TRAINERS IN MY GYM TO HONE MY SKILLS AND CHALLENGE YOU AGAIN, BECAUSE IT TRULY IS MY QUEST TO BREAK YOUR UNBEATEN RECORD ONCE AND FOR ALL!
LEON HAD ANOTHER CHALLENGER IN THE STANDS . . .
NO, THAT'S MY JOB! I'M GONNA BEAT LEON AND BECOME THE GREATEST POKÉMON TRAINER WHO EVER LIVED—YOU'LL SEE!
PIKA!
IF IT ISN'T ASH! SURE! I'LL BE WAITING!
HEE HEE HEE!
PIIIKA!

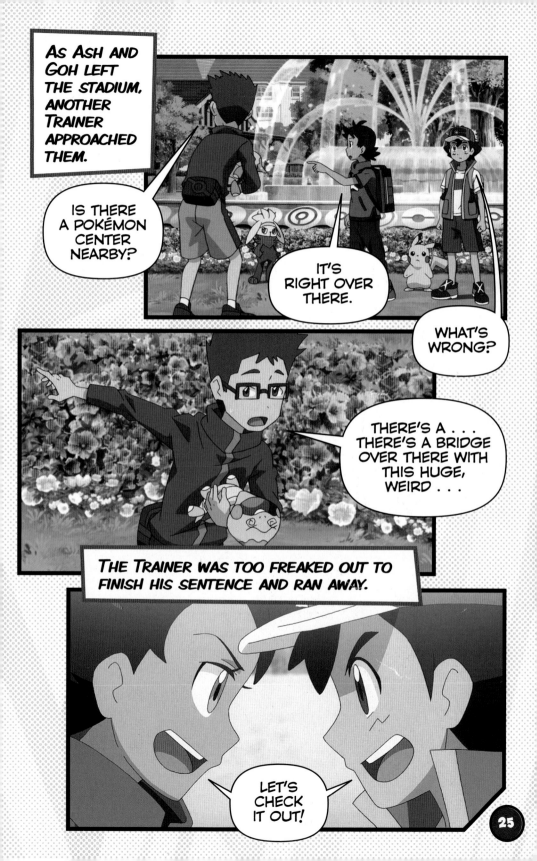

As Ash and Goh left the stadium, another Trainer approached them.

IS THERE A POKÉMON CENTER NEARBY?

IT'S RIGHT OVER THERE.

WHAT'S WRONG?

THERE'S A . . . THERE'S A BRIDGE OVER THERE WITH THIS HUGE, WEIRD . . .

The Trainer was too freaked out to finish his sentence and ran away.

LET'S CHECK IT OUT!

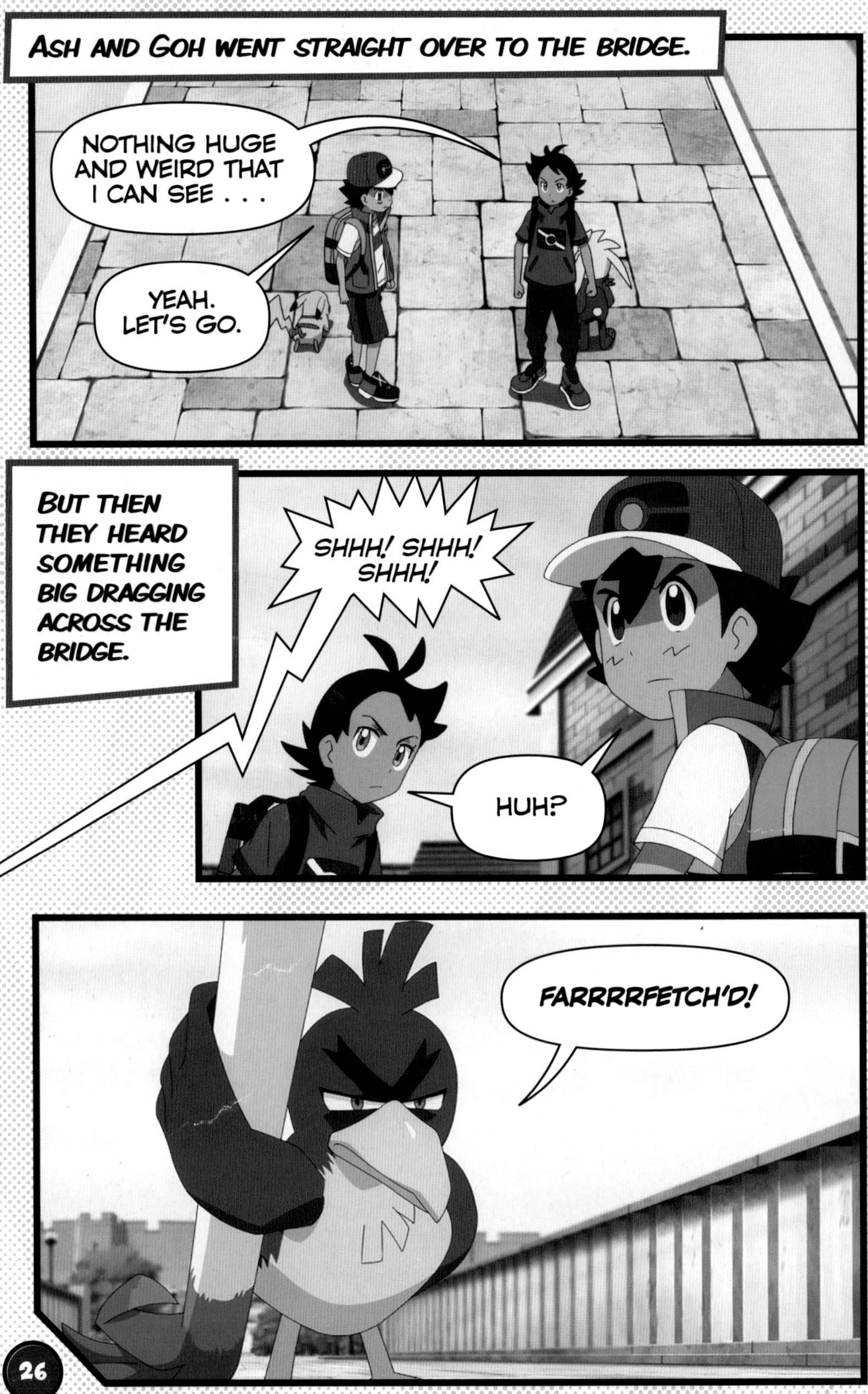
ASH AND GOH WENT STRAIGHT OVER TO THE BRIDGE.
NOTHING HUGE AND WEIRD THAT I CAN SEE . . .
YEAH. LET'S GO.
BUT THEN THEY HEARD SOMETHING BIG DRAGGING ACROSS THE BRIDGE.
SHHH! SHHH! SHHH!
HUH?
FARRRRFETCH'D!

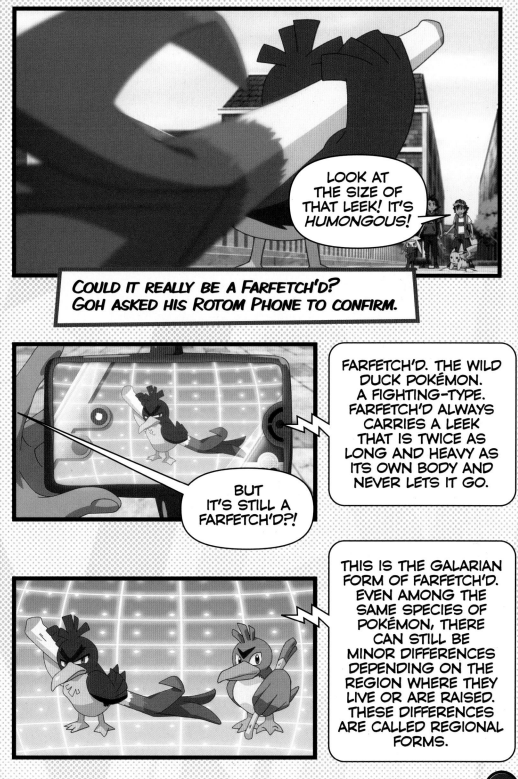

LOOK AT THE SIZE OF THAT LEEK! IT'S HUMONGOUS!

COULD IT REALLY BE A FARFETCH'D? GOH ASKED HIS ROTOM PHONE TO CONFIRM.

FARFETCH'D. THE WILD DUCK POKÉMON. A FIGHTING-TYPE. FARFETCH'D ALWAYS CARRIES A LEEK THAT IS TWICE AS LONG AND HEAVY AS ITS OWN BODY AND NEVER LETS IT GO.

BUT IT'S STILL A FARFETCH'D?!

THIS IS THE GALARIAN FORM OF FARFETCH'D. EVEN AMONG THE SAME SPECIES OF POKÉMON, THERE CAN STILL BE MINOR DIFFERENCES DEPENDING ON THE REGION WHERE THEY LIVE OR ARE RAISED. THESE DIFFERENCES ARE CALLED REGIONAL FORMS.

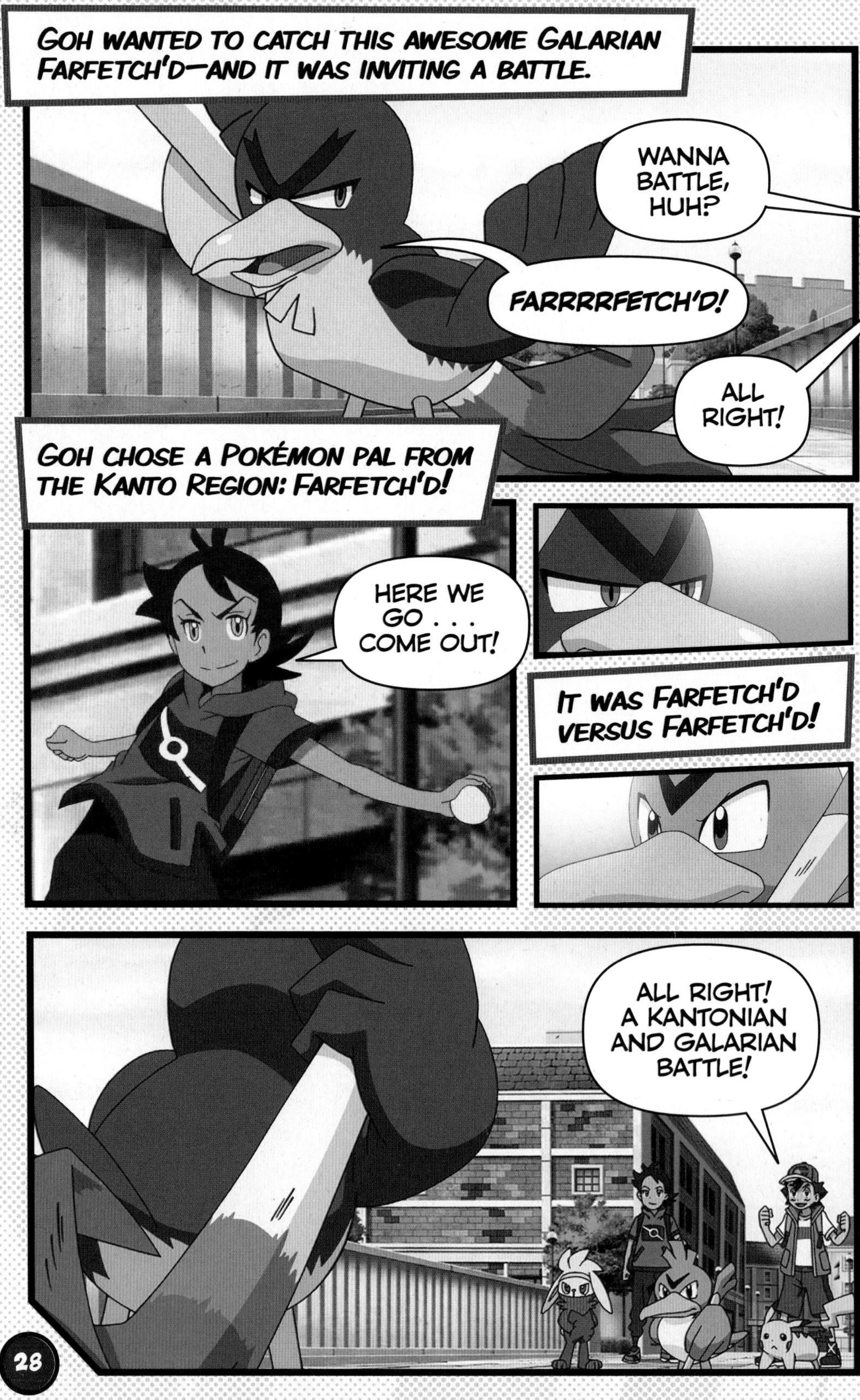
GOH WANTED TO CATCH THIS AWESOME GALARIAN FARFETCH'D—AND IT WAS INVITING A BATTLE.
WANNA BATTLE, HUH?
FARRRRFETCH'D!
ALL RIGHT!
GOH CHOSE A POKÉMON PAL FROM THE KANTO REGION: FARFETCH'D!
HERE WE GO . . . COME OUT!
IT WAS FARFETCH'D VERSUS FARFETCH'D!
ALL RIGHT! A KANTONIAN AND GALARIAN BATTLE!

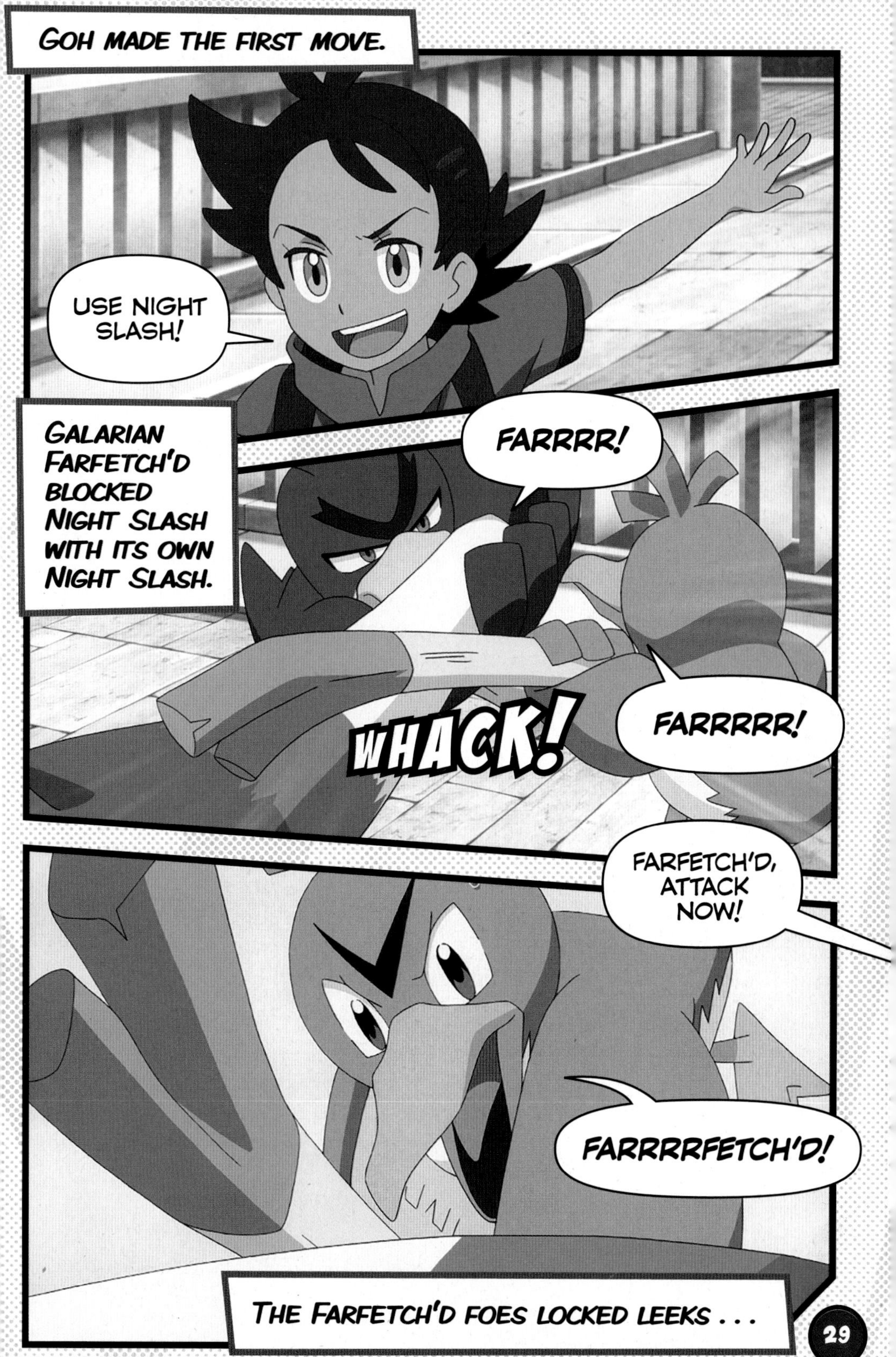
GOH MADE THE FIRST MOVE.
USE NIGHT SLASH!
GALARIAN FARFETCH'D BLOCKED NIGHT SLASH WITH ITS OWN NIGHT SLASH.
FARRRR!
WHACK!
FARRRRR!
FARFETCH'D, ATTACK NOW!
FARRRRFETCH'D!
THE FARFETCH'D FOES LOCKED LEEKS . . .

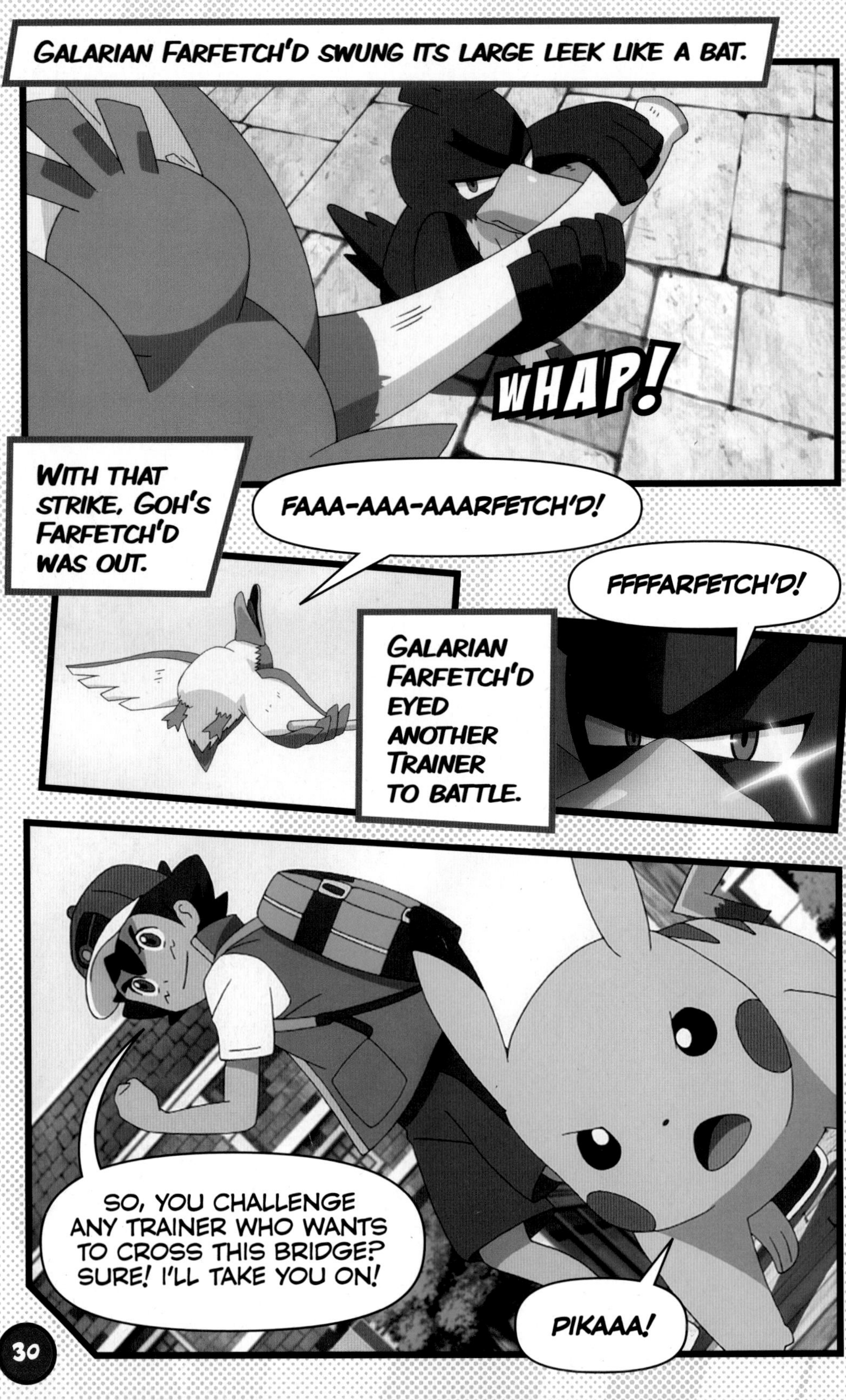
GALARIAN FARFETCH'D SWUNG ITS LARGE LEEK LIKE A BAT.
WHAP!
WITH THAT STRIKE, GOH'S FARFETCH'D WAS OUT.
FAAA-AAA-AAARFETCH'D!
GALARIAN FARFETCH'D EYED ANOTHER TRAINER TO BATTLE.
FFFFARFETCH'D!
SO, YOU CHALLENGE ANY TRAINER WHO WANTS TO CROSS THIS BRIDGE? SURE! I'LL TAKE YOU ON!
PIKAAA!

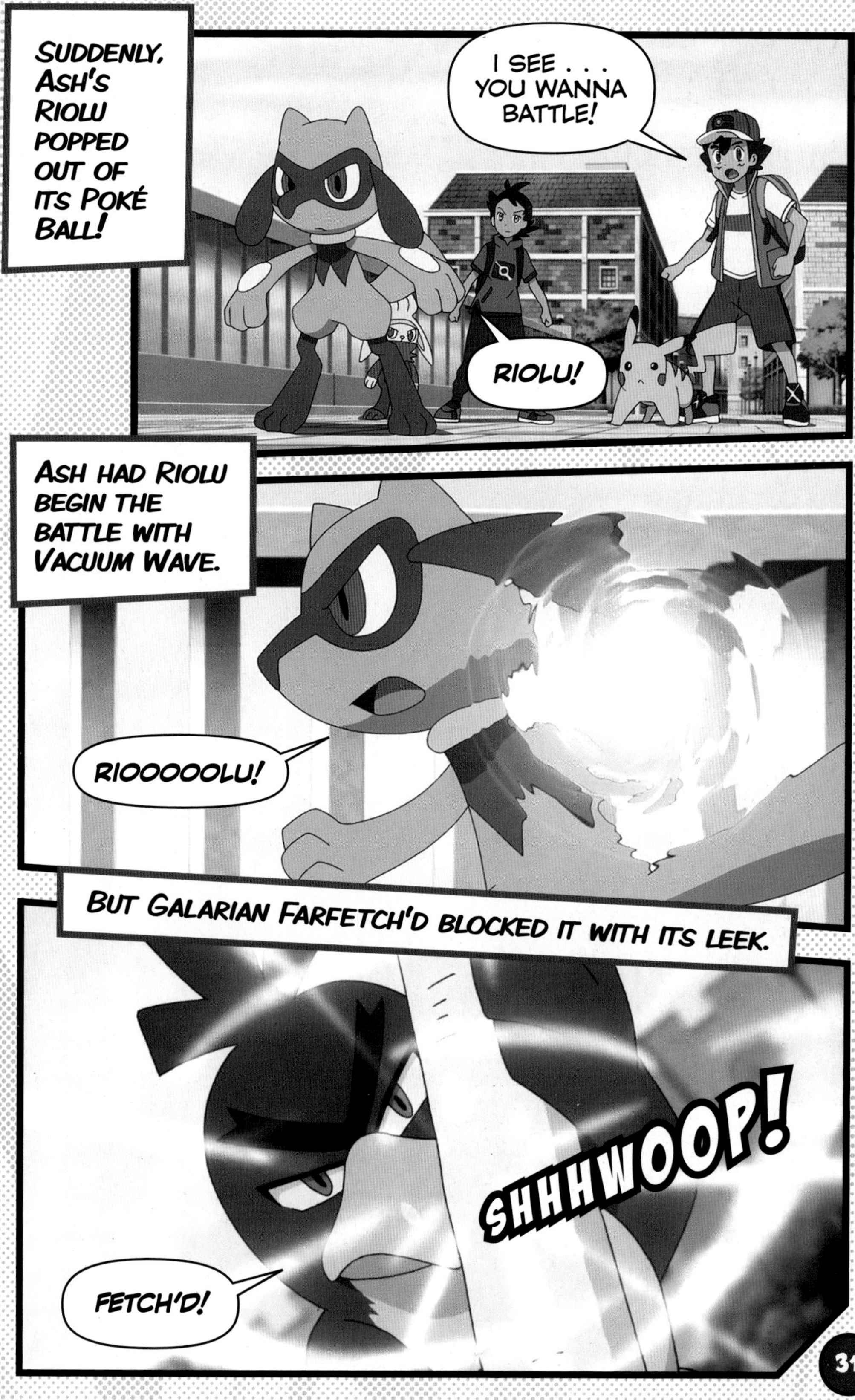
SUDDENLY, ASH'S RIOLU POPPED OUT OF ITS POKÉ BALL!
I SEE . . . YOU WANNA BATTLE!
RIOLU!
ASH HAD RIOLU BEGIN THE BATTLE WITH VACUUM WAVE.
RIOOOOOLU!
BUT GALARIAN FARFETCH'D BLOCKED IT WITH ITS LEEK.
SHHHWOOP!
FETCH'D!

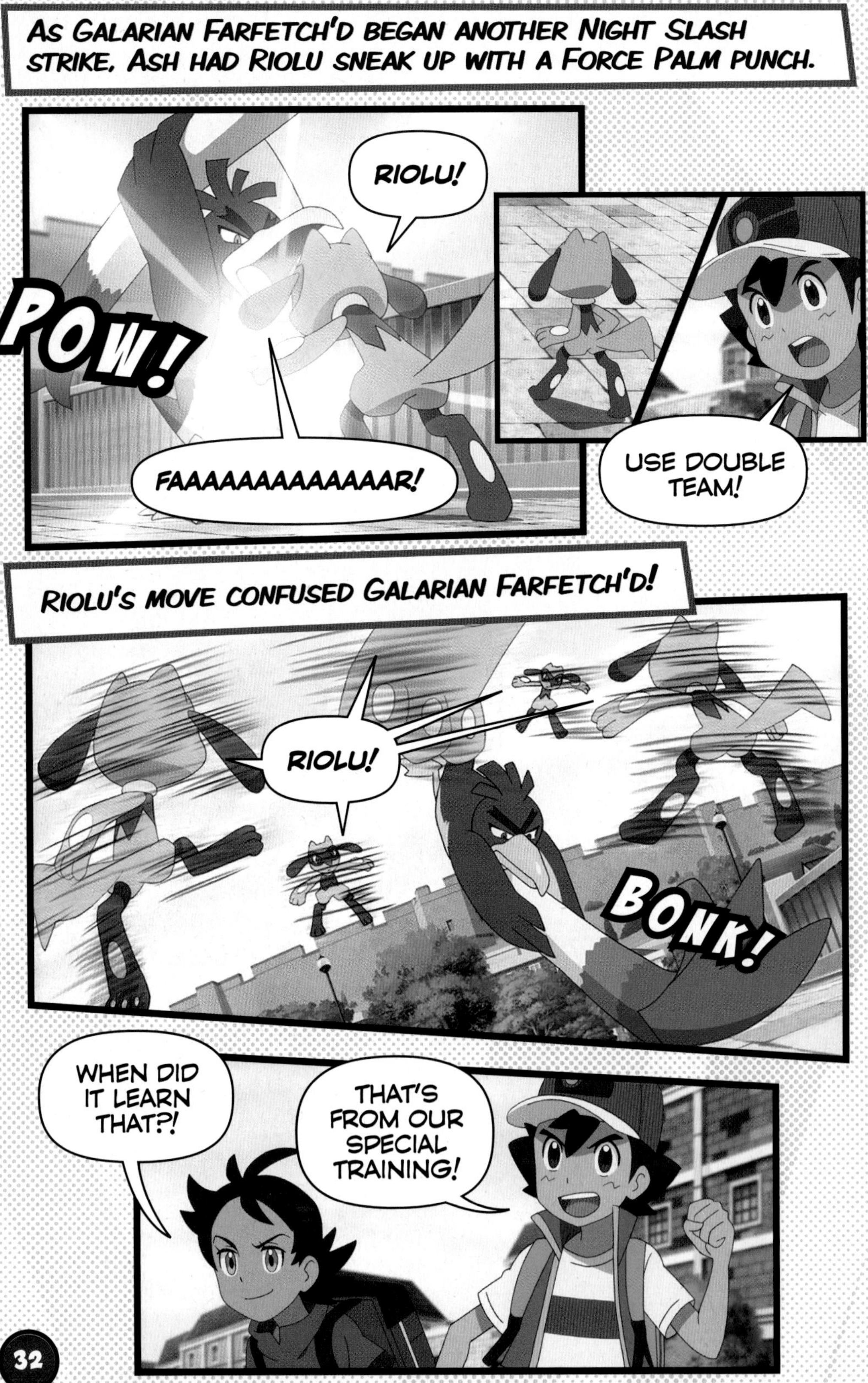
AS GALARIAN FARFETCH'D BEGAN ANOTHER NIGHT SLASH STRIKE, ASH HAD RIOLU SNEAK UP WITH A FORCE PALM PUNCH.
RIOLU!
POW!
FAAAAAAAAAAAAAR!
USE DOUBLE TEAM!
RIOLU'S MOVE CONFUSED GALARIAN FARFETCH'D!
RIOLU!
BONK!
WHEN DID IT LEARN THAT?!
THAT'S FROM OUR SPECIAL TRAINING!

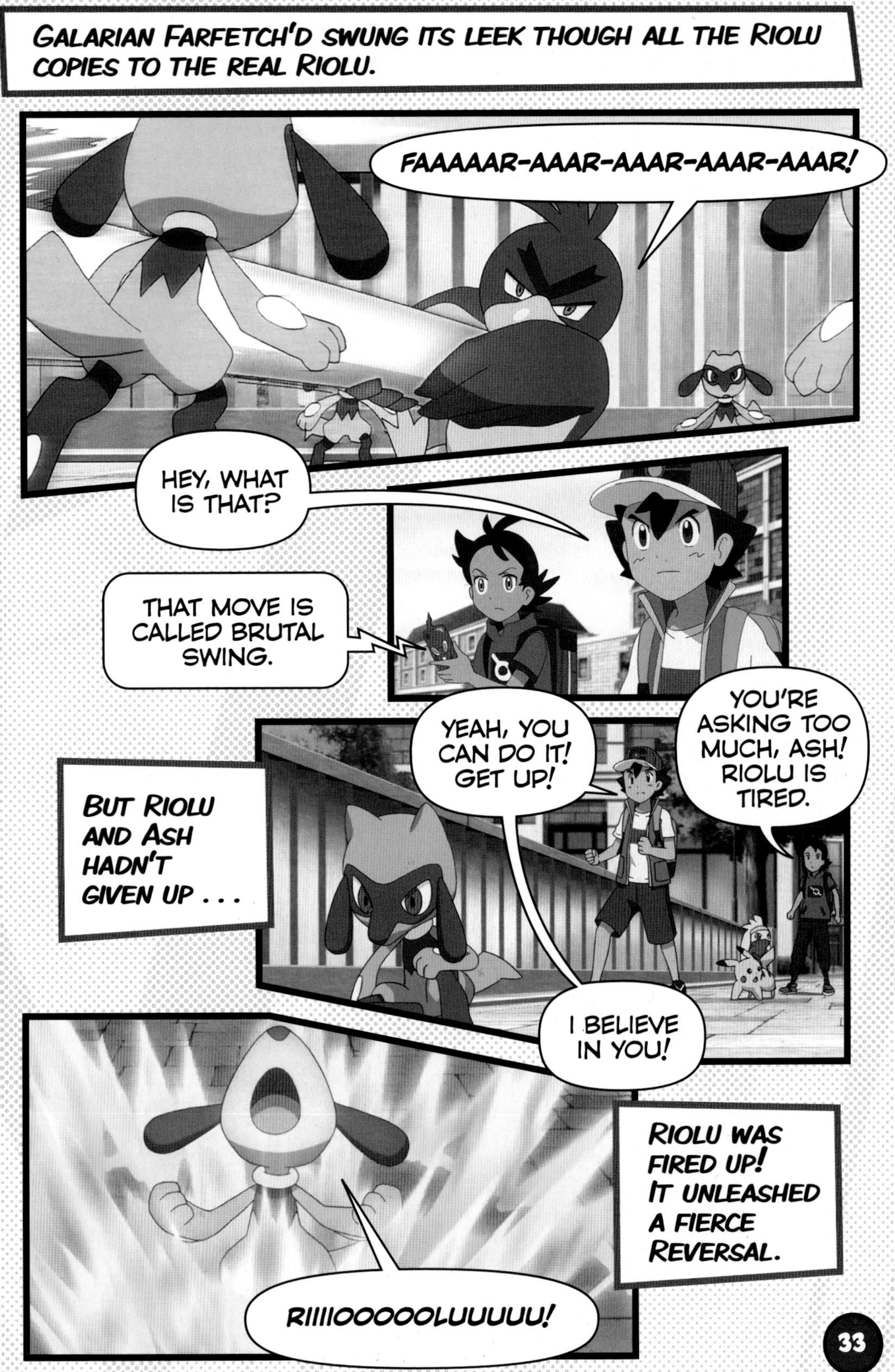
GALARIAN FARFETCH'D SWUNG ITS LEEK THOUGH ALL THE RIOLU COPIES TO THE REAL RIOLU.
FAAAAAR-AAAR-AAAR-AAAR-AAAR!
HEY, WHAT IS THAT?
THAT MOVE IS CALLED BRUTAL SWING.
BUT RIOLU AND ASH HADN'T GIVEN UP . . .
YEAH, YOU CAN DO IT! GET UP!
YOU'RE ASKING TOO MUCH, ASH! RIOLU IS TIRED.
I BELIEVE IN YOU!
RIOLU WAS FIRED UP! IT UNLEASHED A FIERCE REVERSAL.
RIIIOOOOOLUUUUU!

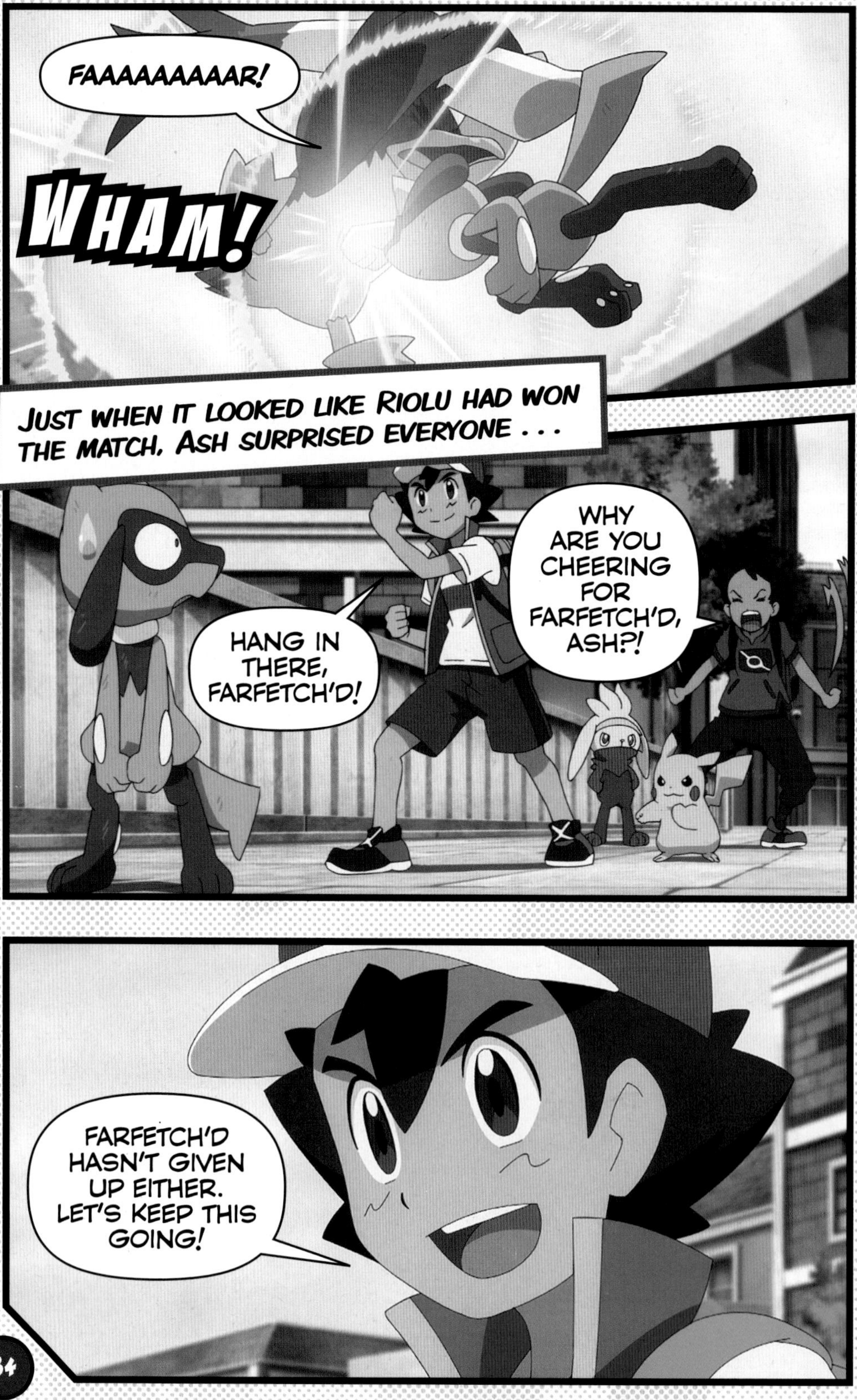
FAAAAAAAAAR!
WHAM!
JUST WHEN IT LOOKED LIKE RIOLU HAD WON THE MATCH, ASH SURPRISED EVERYONE . . .
HANG IN THERE, FARFETCH'D!
WHY ARE YOU CHEERING FOR FARFETCH'D, ASH?!
FARFETCH'D HASN'T GIVEN UP EITHER. LET'S KEEP THIS GOING!

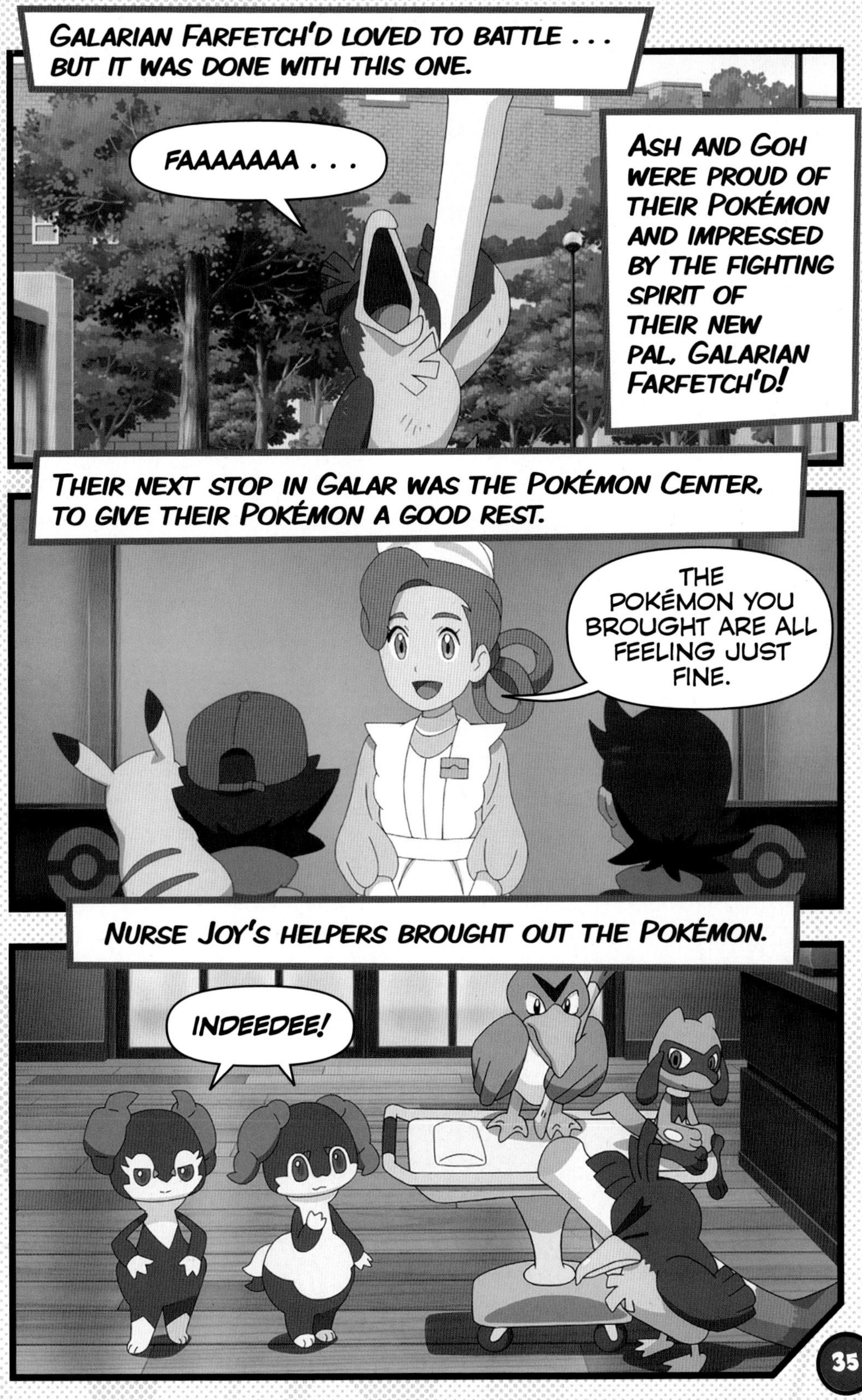
GALARIAN FARFETCH'D LOVED TO BATTLE . . . BUT IT WAS DONE WITH THIS ONE.
FAAAAAAA . . .
ASH AND GOH WERE PROUD OF THEIR POKÉMON AND IMPRESSED BY THE FIGHTING SPIRIT OF THEIR NEW PAL, GALARIAN FARFETCH'D!
THEIR NEXT STOP IN GALAR WAS THE POKÉMON CENTER, TO GIVE THEIR POKÉMON A GOOD REST.
THE POKÉMON YOU BROUGHT ARE ALL FEELING JUST FINE.
NURSE JOY'S HELPERS BROUGHT OUT THE POKÉMON.
INDEEDEE!

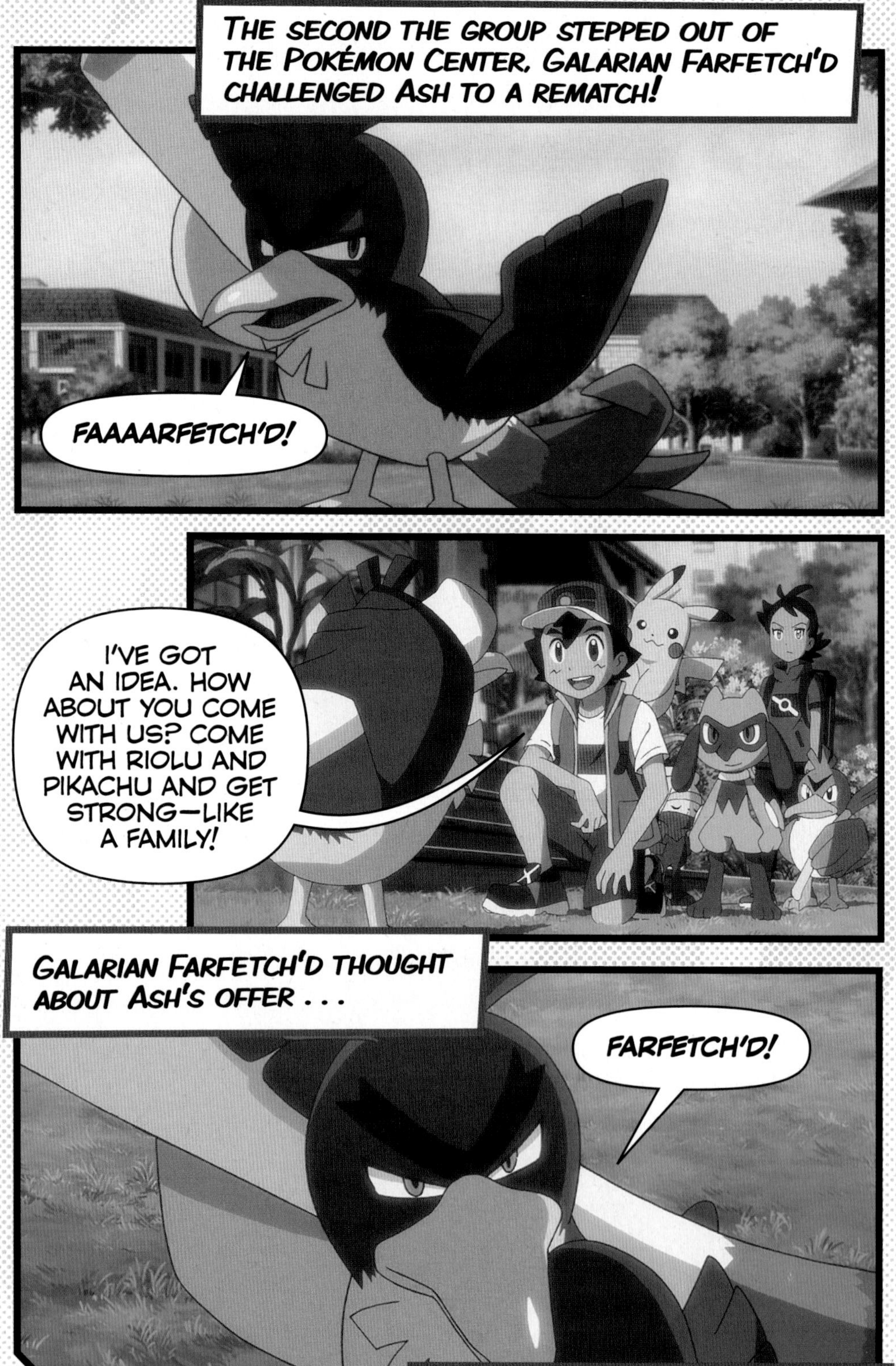
THE SECOND THE GROUP STEPPED OUT OF THE POKÉMON CENTER, GALARIAN FARFETCH'D CHALLENGED ASH TO A REMATCH!
FAAAARFETCH'D!
I'VE GOT AN IDEA. HOW ABOUT YOU COME WITH US? COME WITH RIOLU AND PIKACHU AND GET STRONG—LIKE A FAMILY!
GALARIAN FARFETCH'D THOUGHT ABOUT ASH'S OFFER . . .
FARFETCH'D!
AND DECIDED TO JOIN HIS CREW.

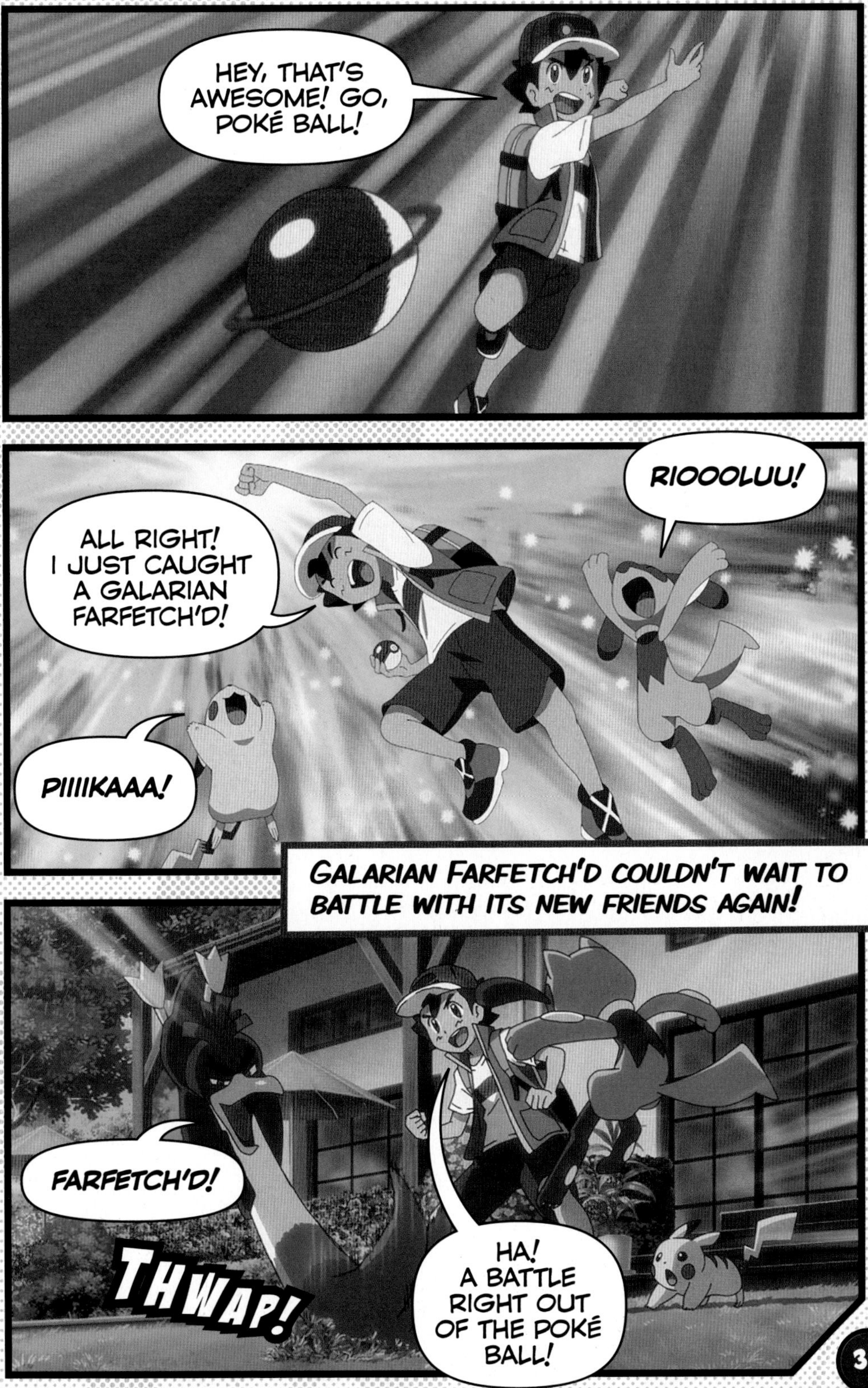
HEY, THAT'S AWESOME! GO, POKÉ BALL!
ALL RIGHT! I JUST CAUGHT A GALARIAN FARFETCH'D!
RIOOOLUU!
PIIIIKAAA!
GALARIAN FARFETCH'D COULDN'T WAIT TO BATTLE WITH ITS NEW FRIENDS AGAIN!
FARFETCH'D!
THWAP!
HA! A BATTLE RIGHT OUT OF THE POKÉ BALL!

# Story 2: Pikachu in Peril

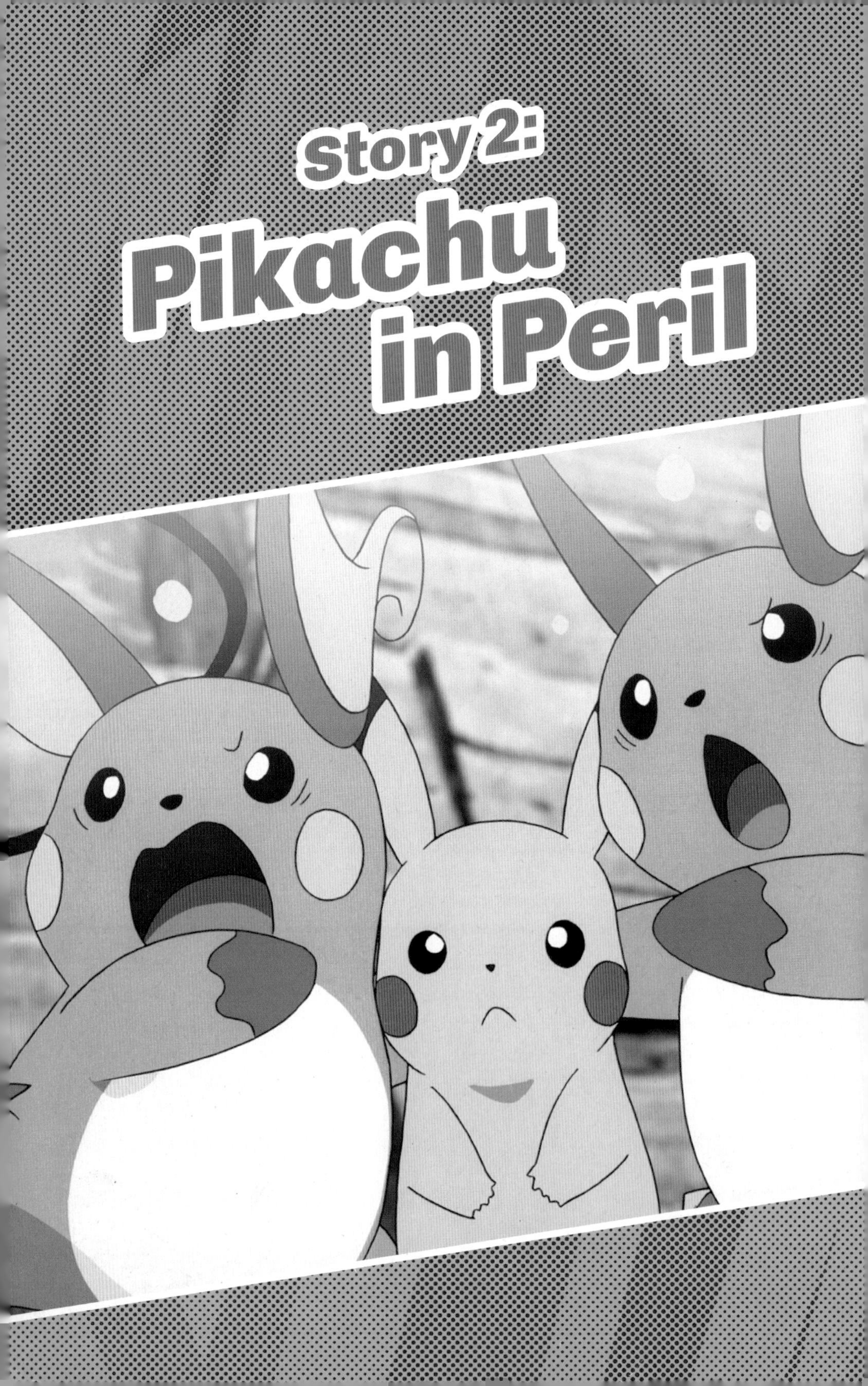

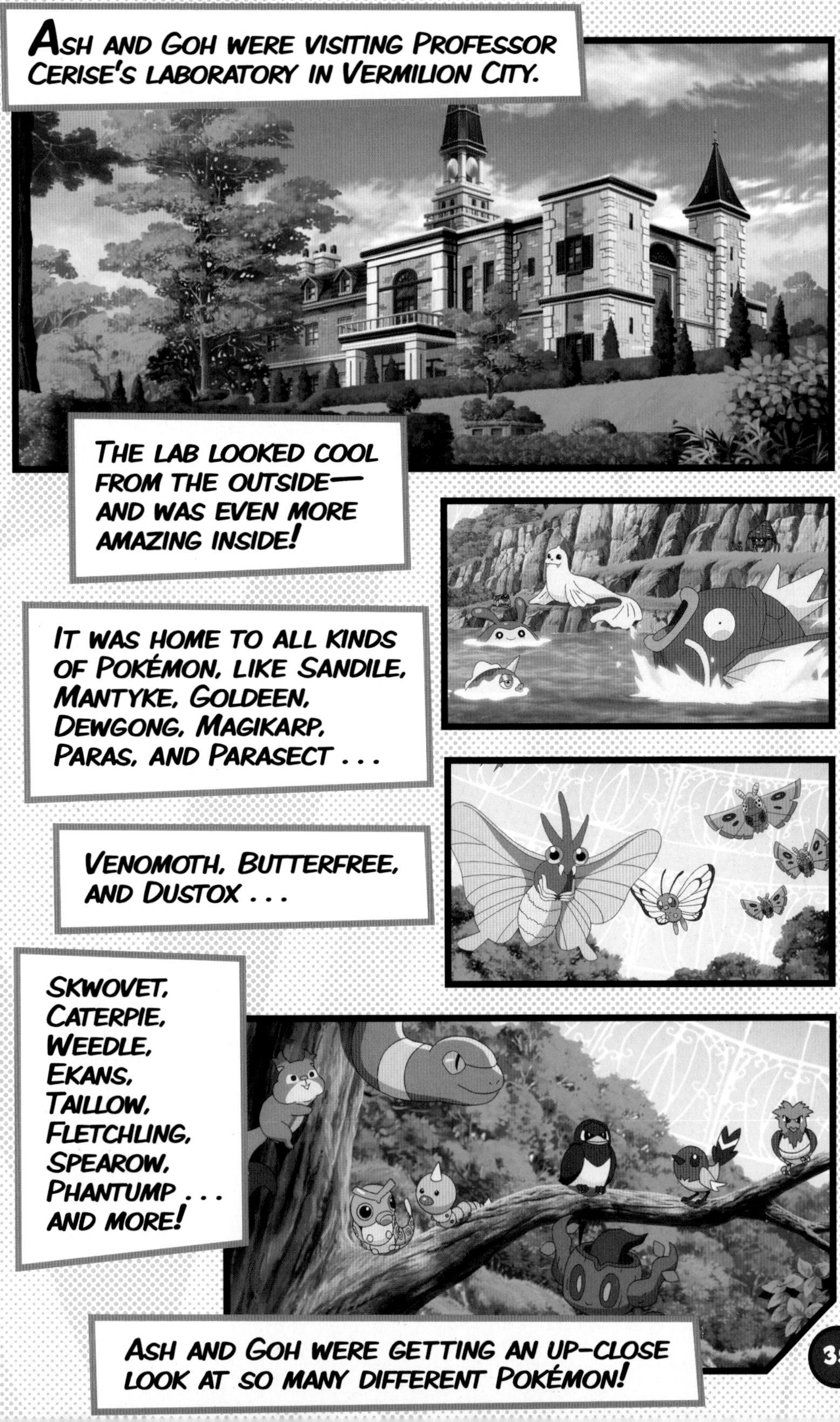

ASH AND GOH WERE VISITING PROFESSOR CERISE'S LABORATORY IN VERMILION CITY.
THE LAB LOOKED COOL FROM THE OUTSIDE—AND WAS EVEN MORE AMAZING INSIDE!
IT WAS HOME TO ALL KINDS OF POKÉMON, LIKE SANDILE, MANTYKE, GOLDEEN, DEWGONG, MAGIKARP, PARAS, AND PARASECT . . .
VENOMOTH, BUTTERFREE, AND DUSTOX . . .
SKWOVET, CATERPIE, WEEDLE, EKANS, TAILLOW, FLETCHLING, SPEAROW, PHANTUMP . . . AND MORE!
ASH AND GOH WERE GETTING AN UP-CLOSE LOOK AT SO MANY DIFFERENT POKÉMON!

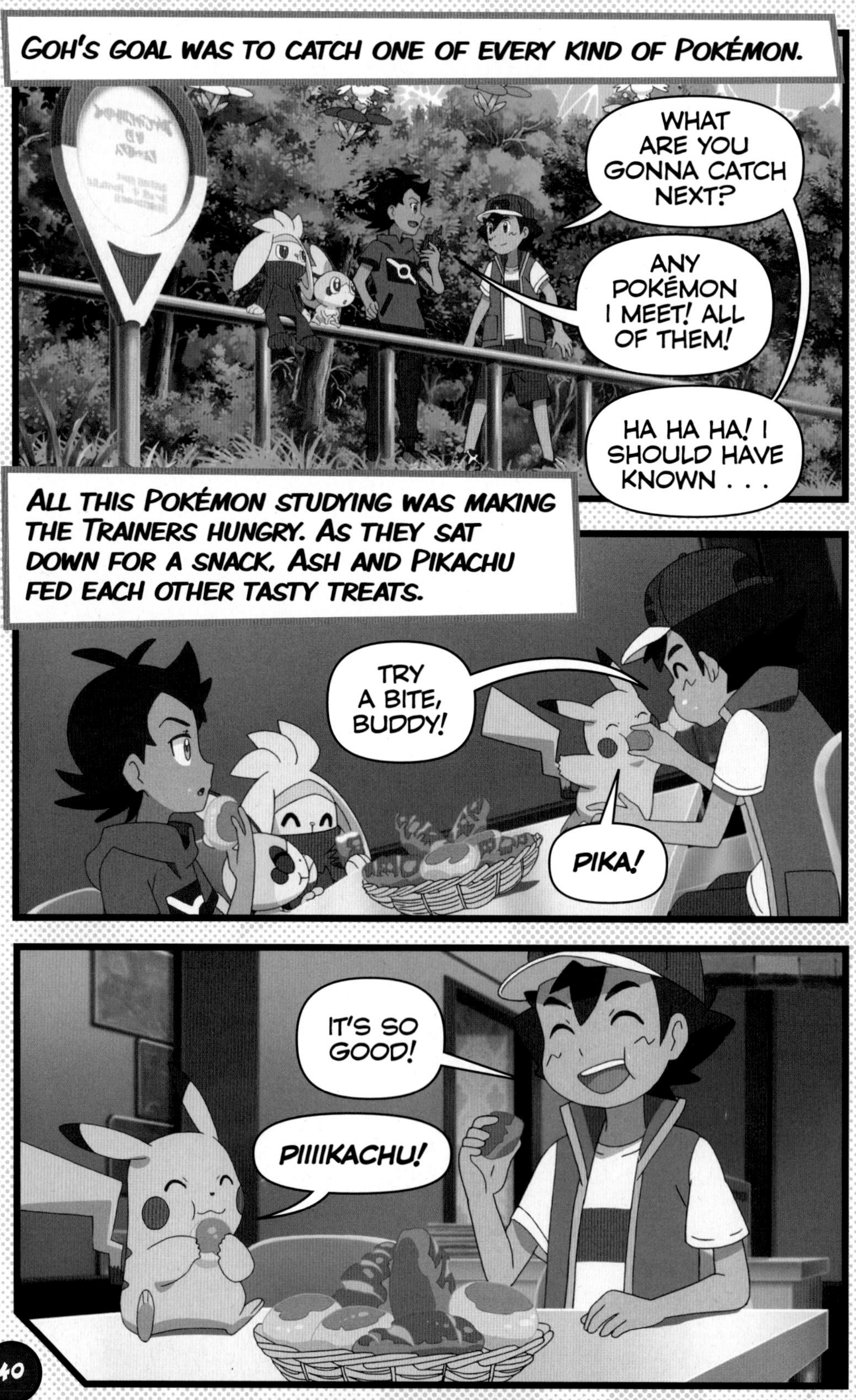
GOH'S GOAL WAS TO CATCH ONE OF EVERY KIND OF POKÉMON.
WHAT ARE YOU GONNA CATCH NEXT?
ANY POKÉMON I MEET! ALL OF THEM!
HA HA HA! I SHOULD HAVE KNOWN . . .
ALL THIS POKÉMON STUDYING WAS MAKING THE TRAINERS HUNGRY. AS THEY SAT DOWN FOR A SNACK, ASH AND PIKACHU FED EACH OTHER TASTY TREATS.
TRY A BITE, BUDDY!
PIKA!
IT'S SO GOOD!
PIIIIKACHU!

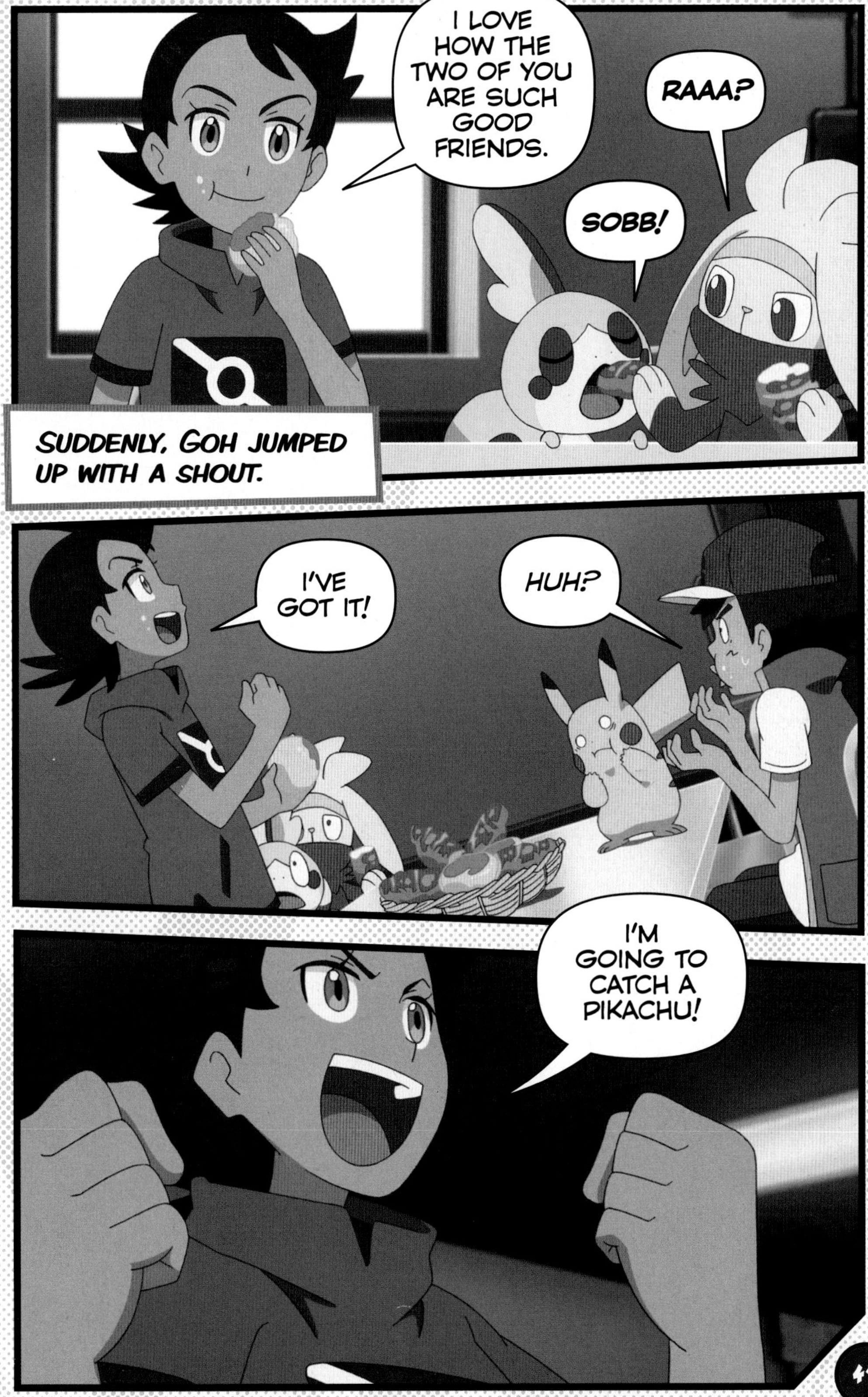
I LOVE HOW THE TWO OF YOU ARE SUCH GOOD FRIENDS.
RAAA?
SOBB!
SUDDENLY, GOH JUMPED UP WITH A SHOUT.
I'VE GOT IT!
HUH?
I'M GOING TO CATCH A PIKACHU!

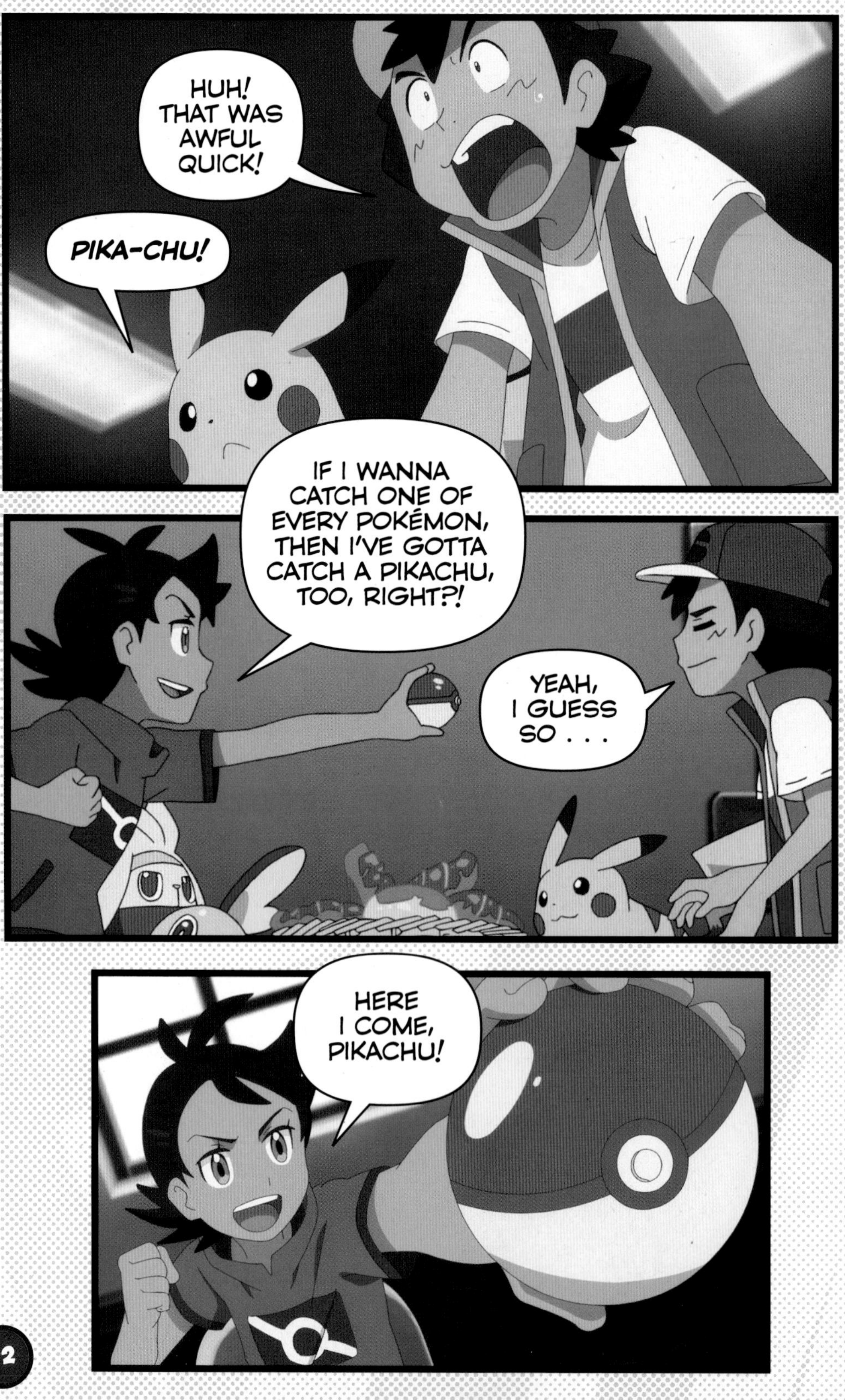
HUH! THAT WAS AWFUL QUICK!
PIKA-CHU!
IF I WANNA CATCH ONE OF EVERY POKÉMON, THEN I'VE GOTTA CATCH A PIKACHU, TOO, RIGHT?!
YEAH, I GUESS SO . . .
HERE I COME, PIKACHU!

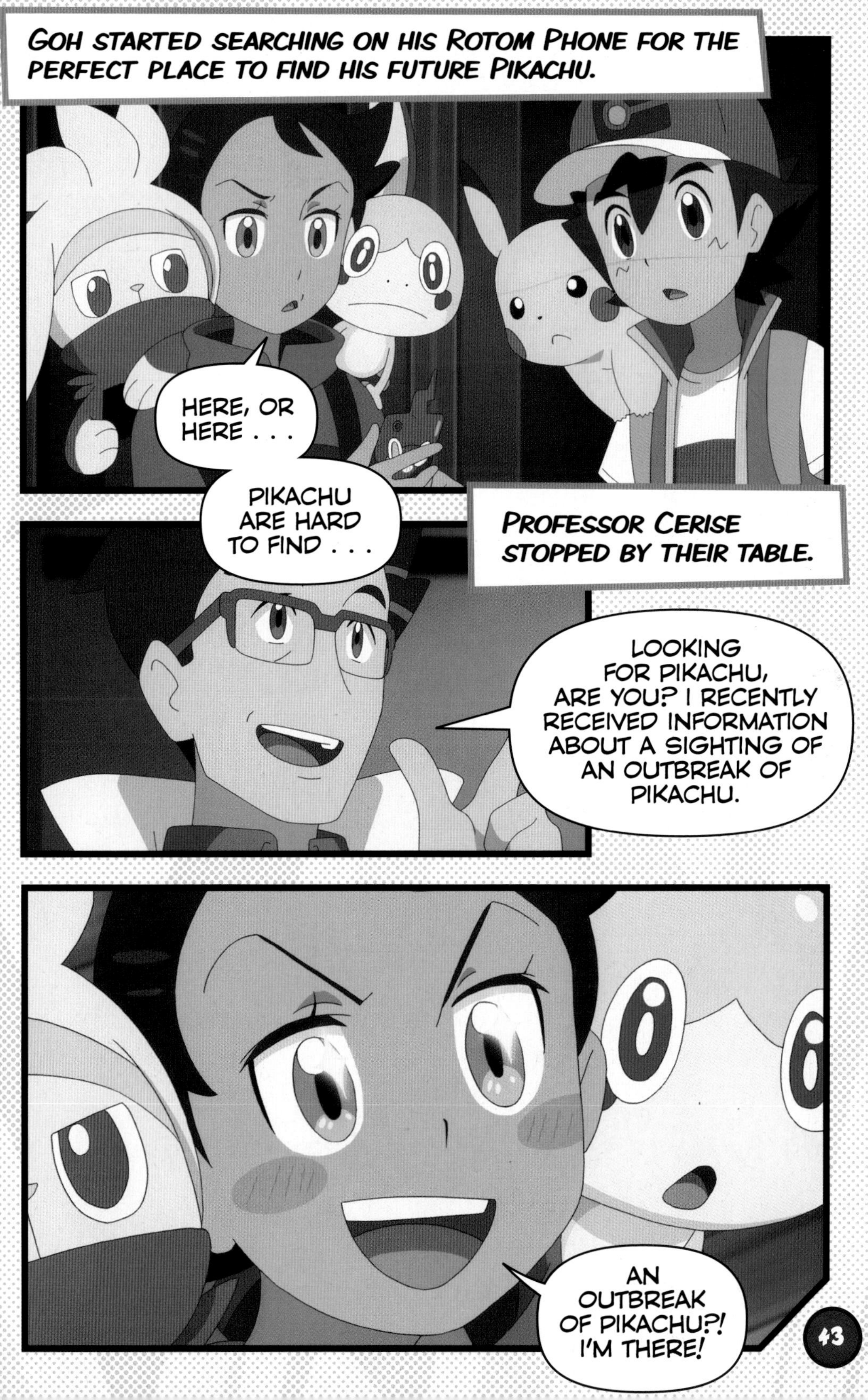
GOH STARTED SEARCHING ON HIS ROTOM PHONE FOR THE PERFECT PLACE TO FIND HIS FUTURE PIKACHU.
HERE, OR HERE . . .
PIKACHU ARE HARD TO FIND . . .
PROFESSOR CERISE STOPPED BY THEIR TABLE.
LOOKING FOR PIKACHU, ARE YOU? I RECENTLY RECEIVED INFORMATION ABOUT A SIGHTING OF AN OUTBREAK OF PIKACHU.
AN OUTBREAK OF PIKACHU?! I'M THERE!

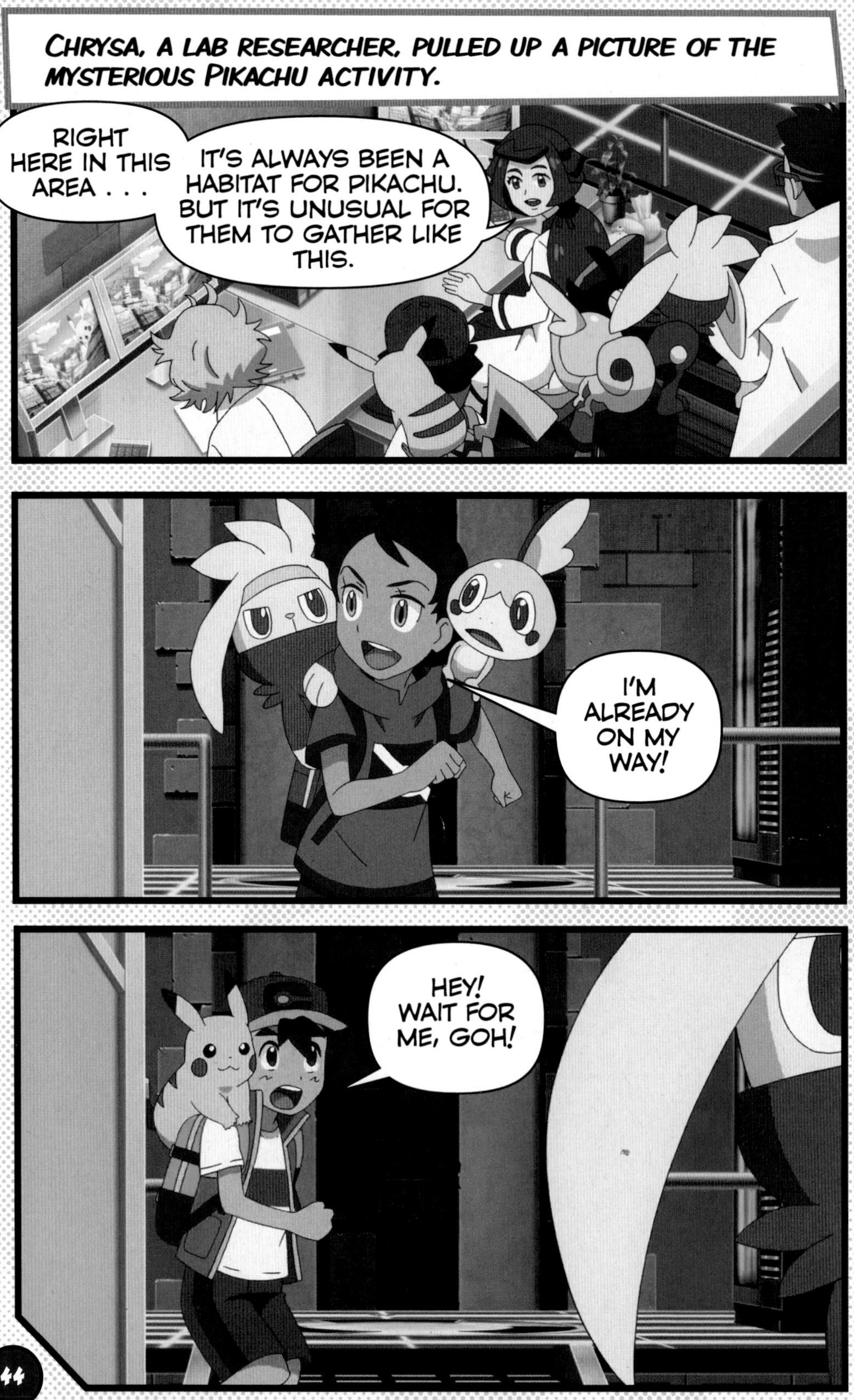
Chrysa, a lab researcher, pulled up a picture of the mysterious Pikachu activity.
RIGHT HERE IN THIS AREA . . .
IT'S ALWAYS BEEN A HABITAT FOR PIKACHU. BUT IT'S UNUSUAL FOR THEM TO GATHER LIKE THIS.
I'M ALREADY ON MY WAY!
HEY! WAIT FOR ME, GOH!

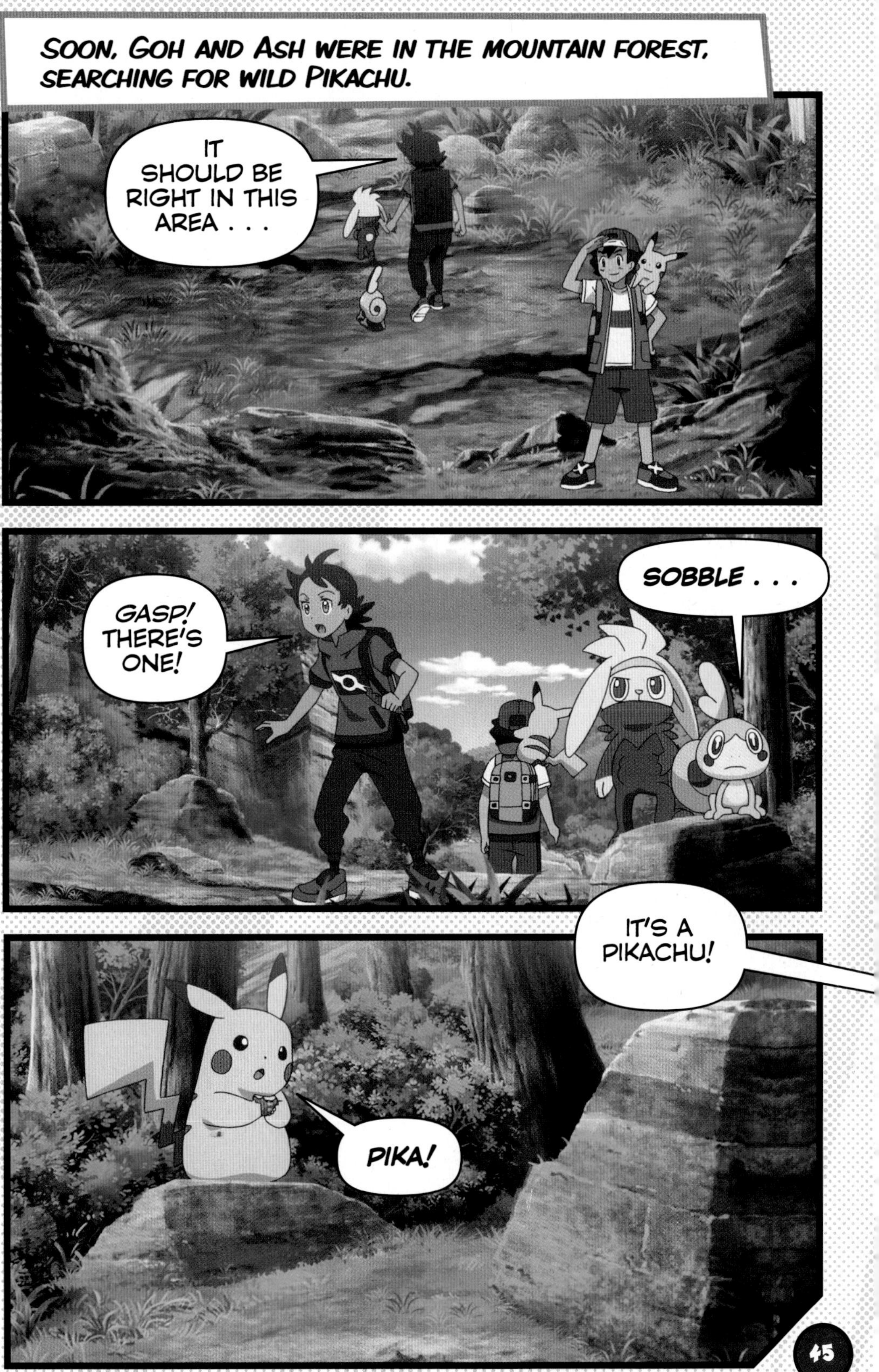
SOON, GOH AND ASH WERE IN THE MOUNTAIN FOREST, SEARCHING FOR WILD PIKACHU.
IT SHOULD BE RIGHT IN THIS AREA . . .
GASP! THERE'S ONE!
SOBBLE . . .
IT'S A PIKACHU!
PIKA!

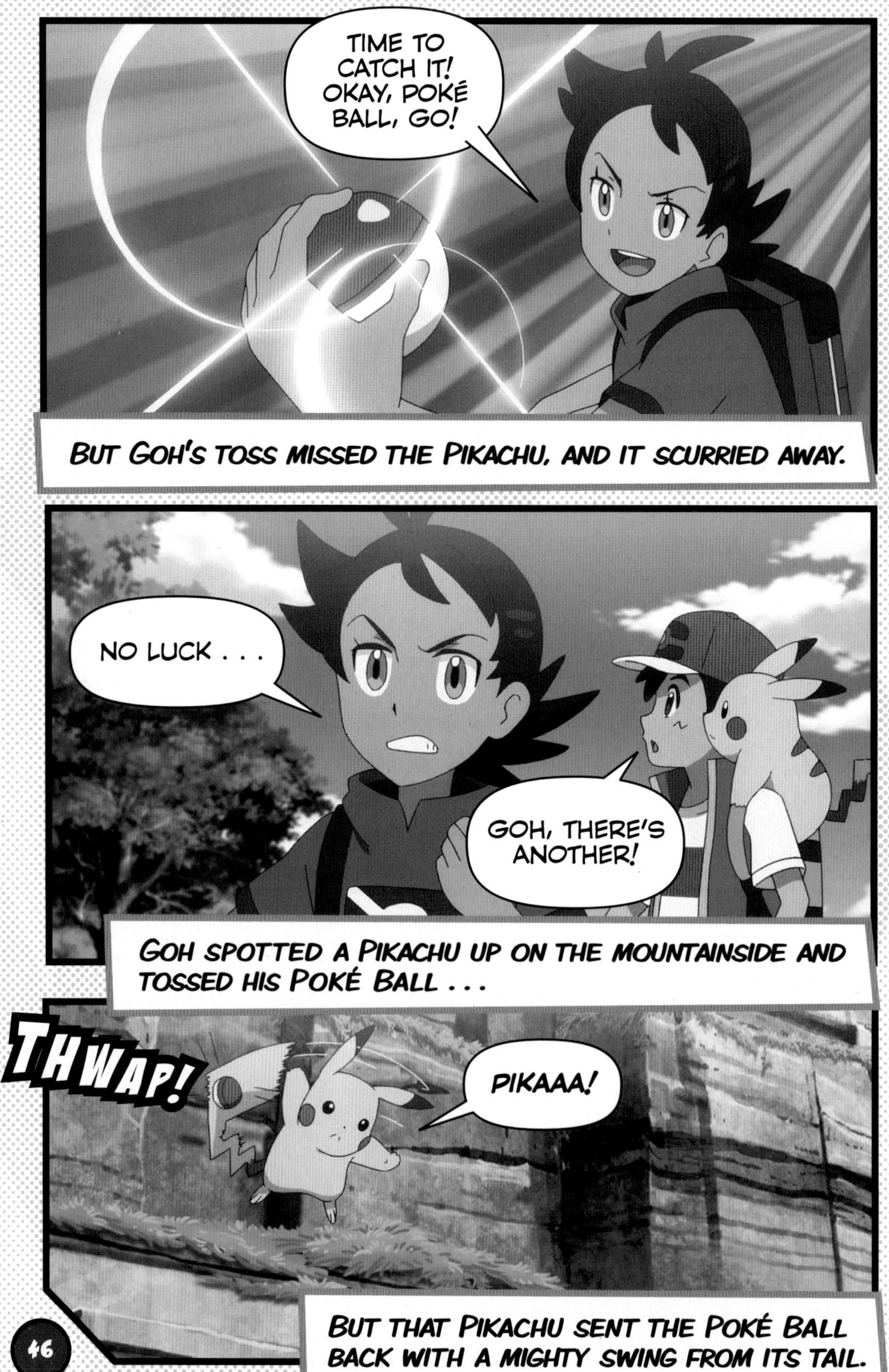
TIME TO CATCH IT! OKAY, POKÉ BALL, GO!
BUT GOH'S TOSS MISSED THE PIKACHU, AND IT SCURRIED AWAY.
NO LUCK . . .
GOH, THERE'S ANOTHER!
GOH SPOTTED A PIKACHU UP ON THE MOUNTAINSIDE AND TOSSED HIS POKÉ BALL . . .
THWAP!
PIKAAA!
BUT THAT PIKACHU SENT THE POKÉ BALL BACK WITH A MIGHTY SWING FROM ITS TAIL.

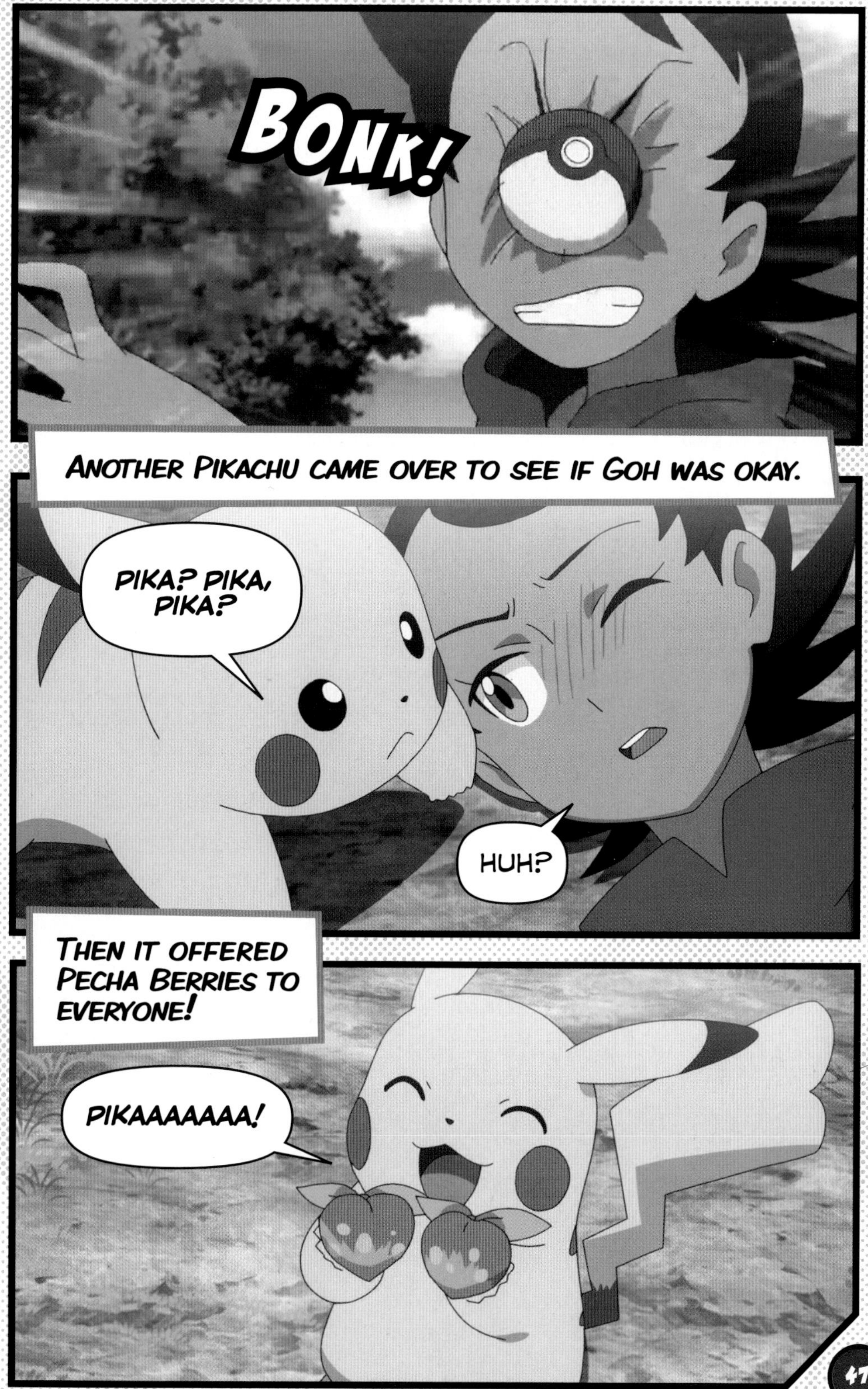
BONK!
ANOTHER PIKACHU CAME OVER TO SEE IF GOH WAS OKAY.
PIKA? PIKA, PIKA?
HUH?
THEN IT OFFERED PECHA BERRIES TO EVERYONE!
PIKAAAAAAAA!

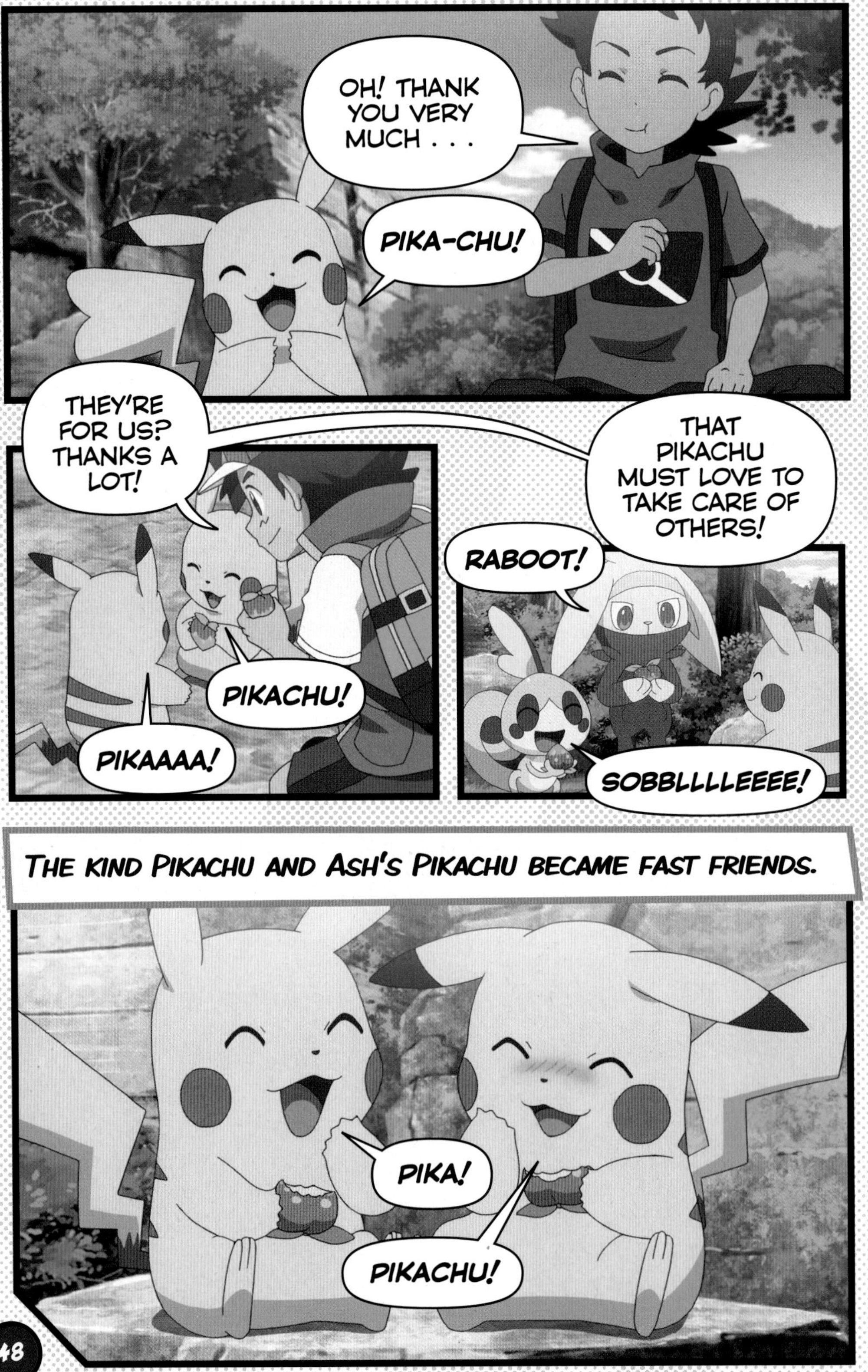
OH! THANK YOU VERY MUCH . . .
PIKA-CHU!
THEY'RE FOR US? THANKS A LOT!
THAT PIKACHU MUST LOVE TO TAKE CARE OF OTHERS!
PIKACHU!
PIKAAAA!
RABOOT!
SOBBLLLLEEEE!
THE KIND PIKACHU AND ASH'S PIKACHU BECAME FAST FRIENDS.
PIKA!
PIKACHU!

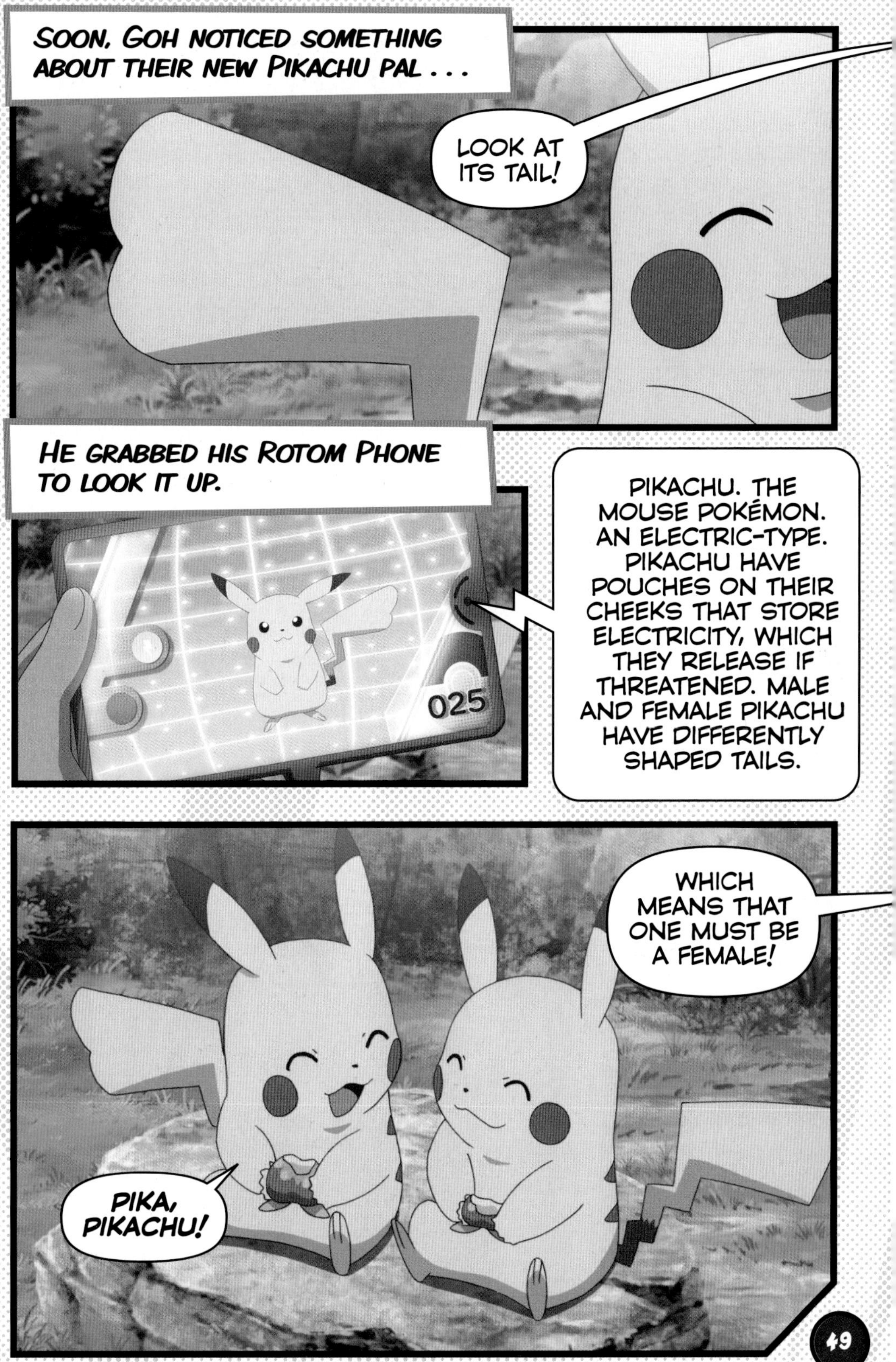
SOON, GOH NOTICED SOMETHING ABOUT THEIR NEW PIKACHU PAL . . .
LOOK AT ITS TAIL!
HE GRABBED HIS ROTOM PHONE TO LOOK IT UP.
025
PIKACHU. THE MOUSE POKÉMON. AN ELECTRIC-TYPE. PIKACHU HAVE POUCHES ON THEIR CHEEKS THAT STORE ELECTRICITY, WHICH THEY RELEASE IF THREATENED. MALE AND FEMALE PIKACHU HAVE DIFFERENTLY SHAPED TAILS.
WHICH MEANS THAT ONE MUST BE A FEMALE!
PIKA, PIKACHU!

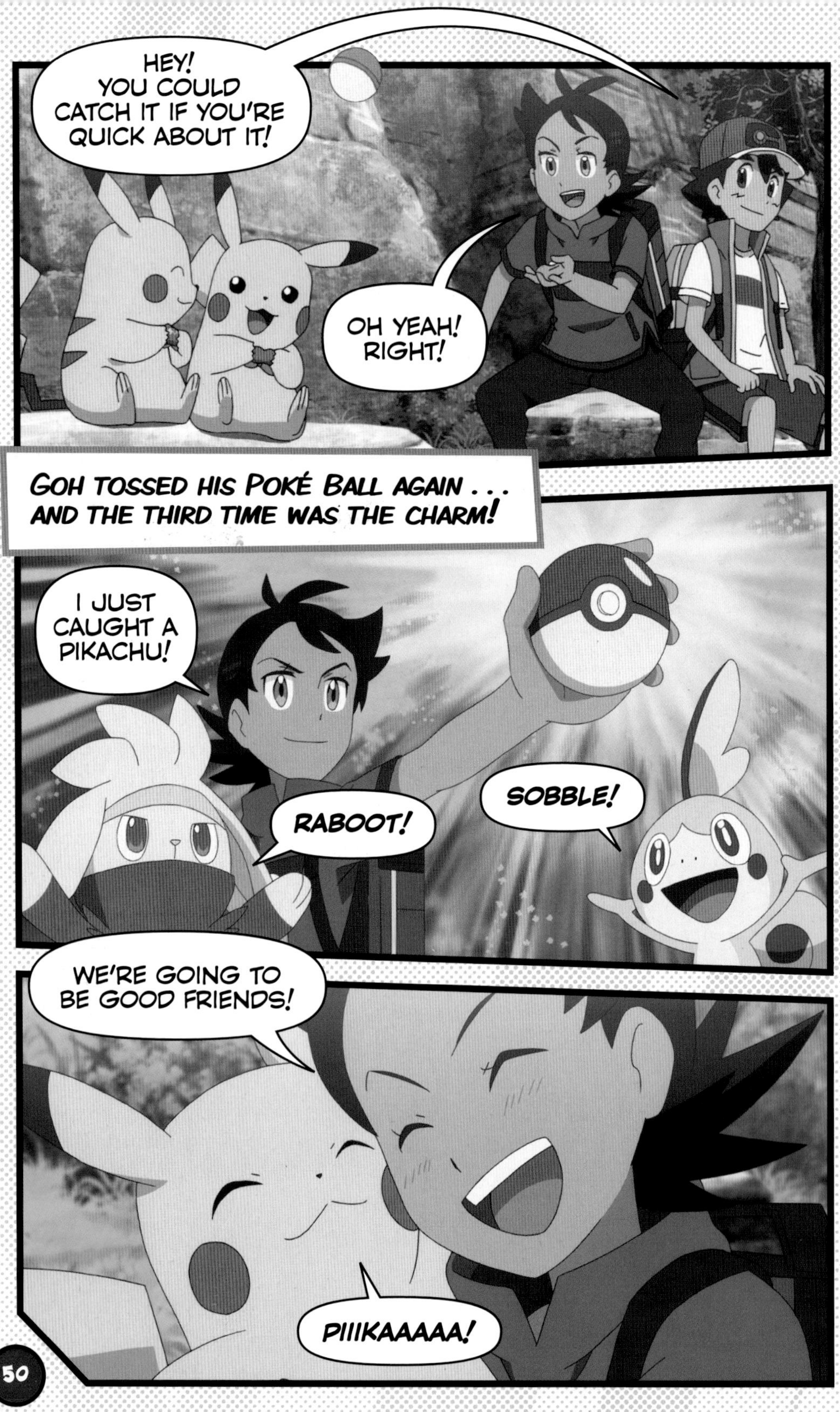
HEY! YOU COULD CATCH IT IF YOU'RE QUICK ABOUT IT!
OH YEAH! RIGHT!
GOH TOSSED HIS POKÉ BALL AGAIN . . . AND THE THIRD TIME WAS THE CHARM!
I JUST CAUGHT A PIKACHU!
RABOOT!
SOBBLE!
WE'RE GOING TO BE GOOD FRIENDS!
PIIIKAAAAA!

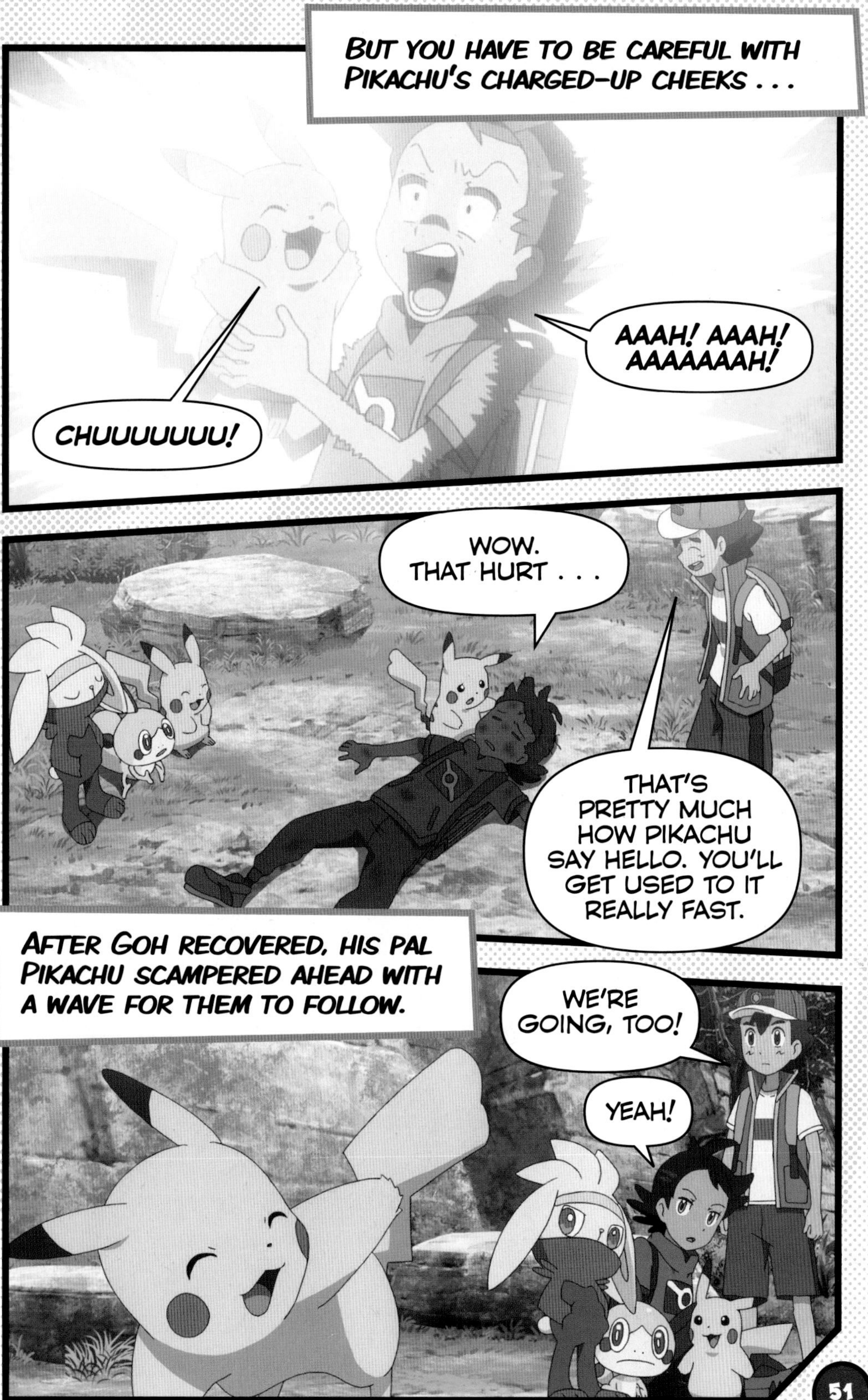

BUT YOU HAVE TO BE CAREFUL WITH PIKACHU'S CHARGED-UP CHEEKS . . .
CHUUUUUUU!
AAAH! AAAH! AAAAAAAH!
WOW. THAT HURT . . .
THAT'S PRETTY MUCH HOW PIKACHU SAY HELLO. YOU'LL GET USED TO IT REALLY FAST.
AFTER GOH RECOVERED, HIS PAL PIKACHU SCAMPERED AHEAD WITH A WAVE FOR THEM TO FOLLOW.
WE'RE GOING, TOO!
YEAH!

THEY COULDN'T BELIEVE WHERE THEY ENDED UP!

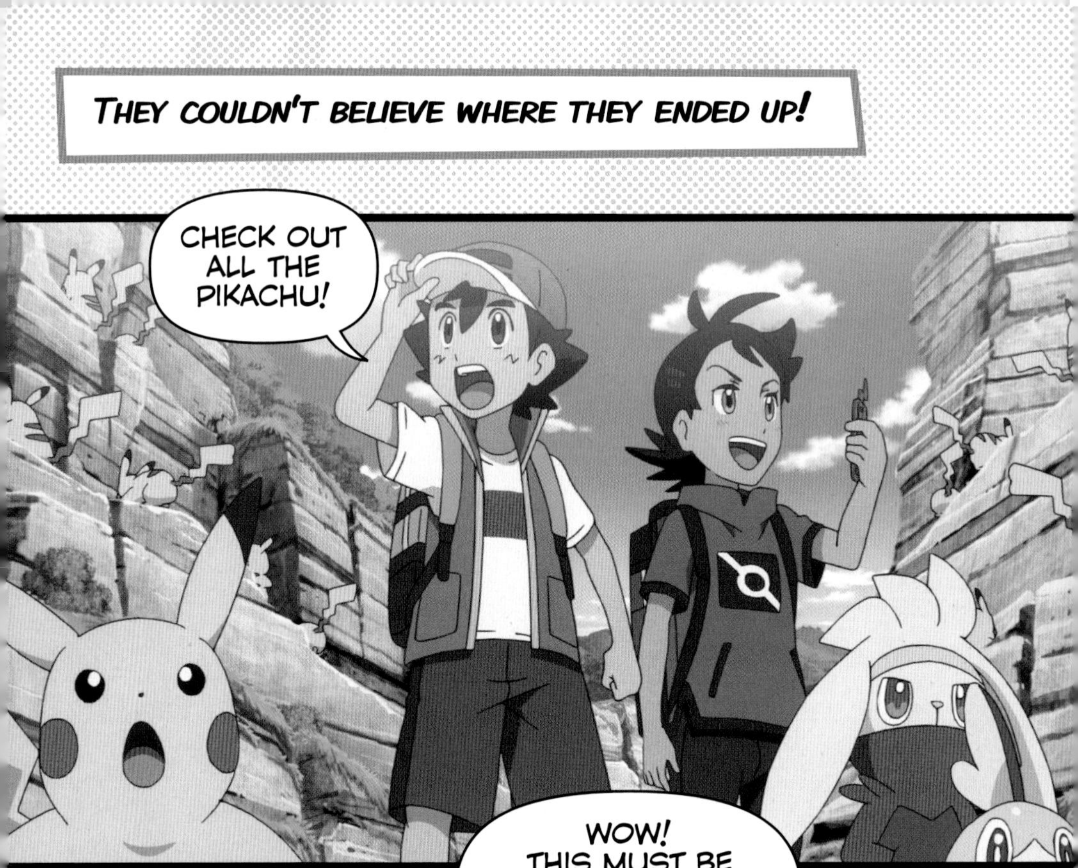
CHECK OUT ALL THE PIKACHU!

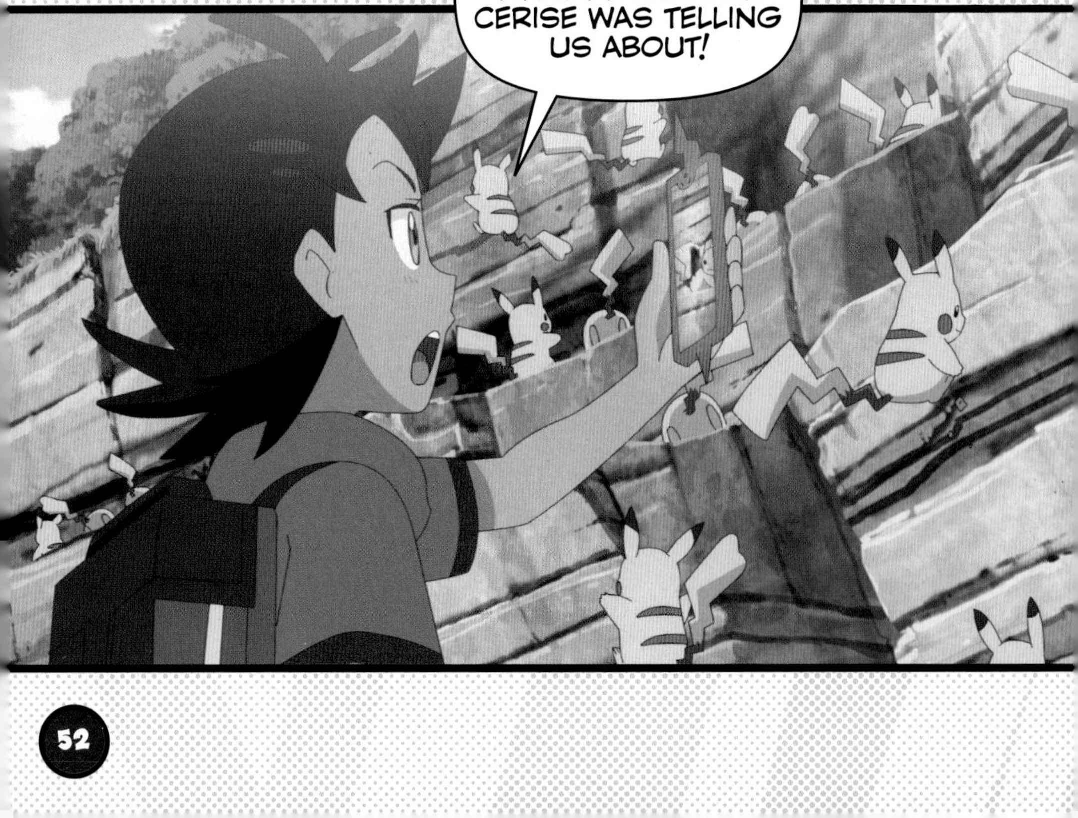
WOW! THIS MUST BE WHAT PROFESSOR CERISE WAS TELLING US ABOUT!

BUT ASH AND GOH WEREN'T THE ONLY PEOPLE NEARBY . . .

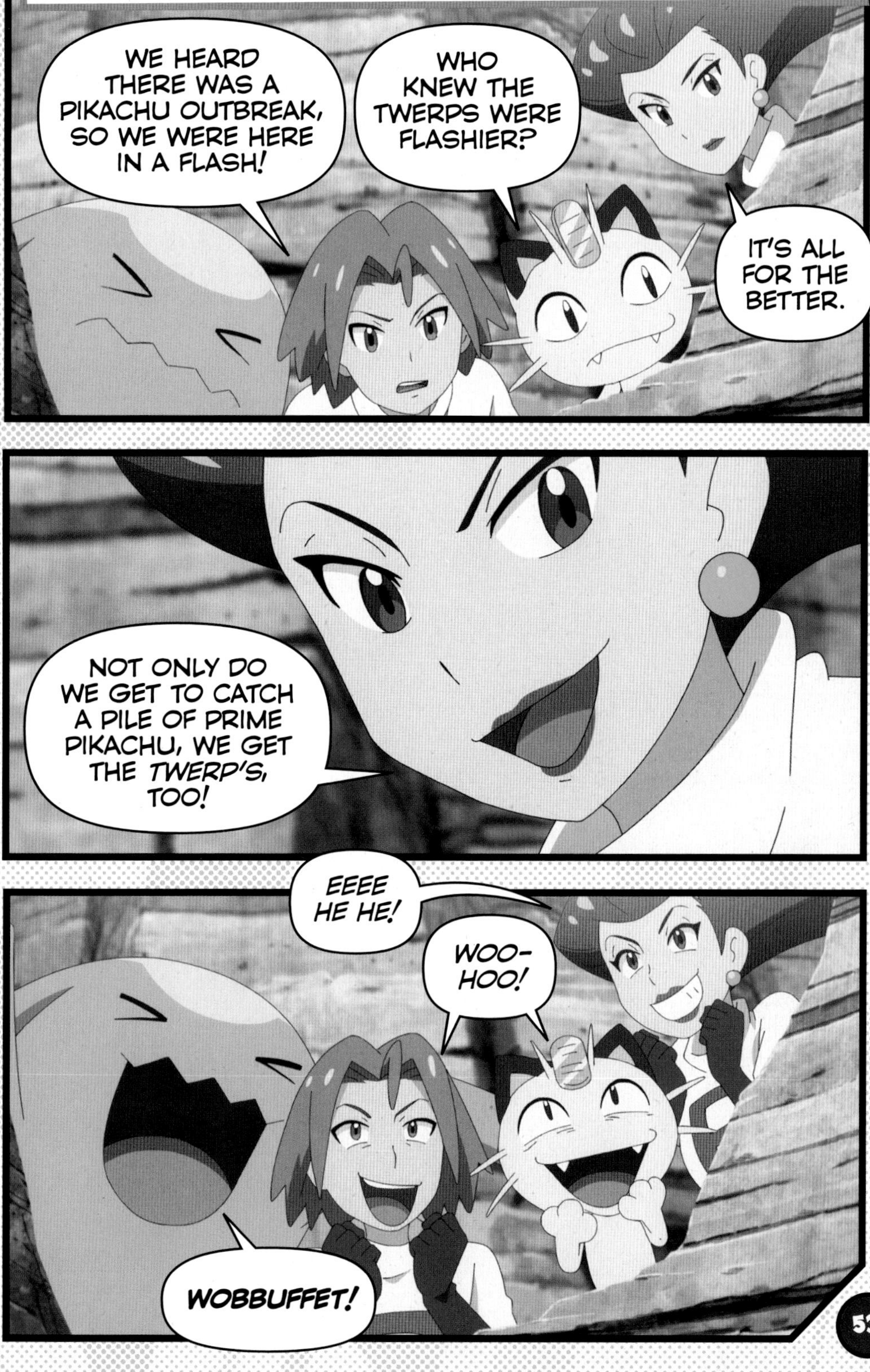
WE HEARD THERE WAS A PIKACHU OUTBREAK, SO WE WERE HERE IN A FLASH!
WHO KNEW THE TWERPS WERE FLASHIER?
IT'S ALL FOR THE BETTER.
NOT ONLY DO WE GET TO CATCH A PILE OF PRIME PIKACHU, WE GET THE *TWERP'S*, TOO!
EEEE HE HE!
WOO-HOO!
WOBBUFFET!

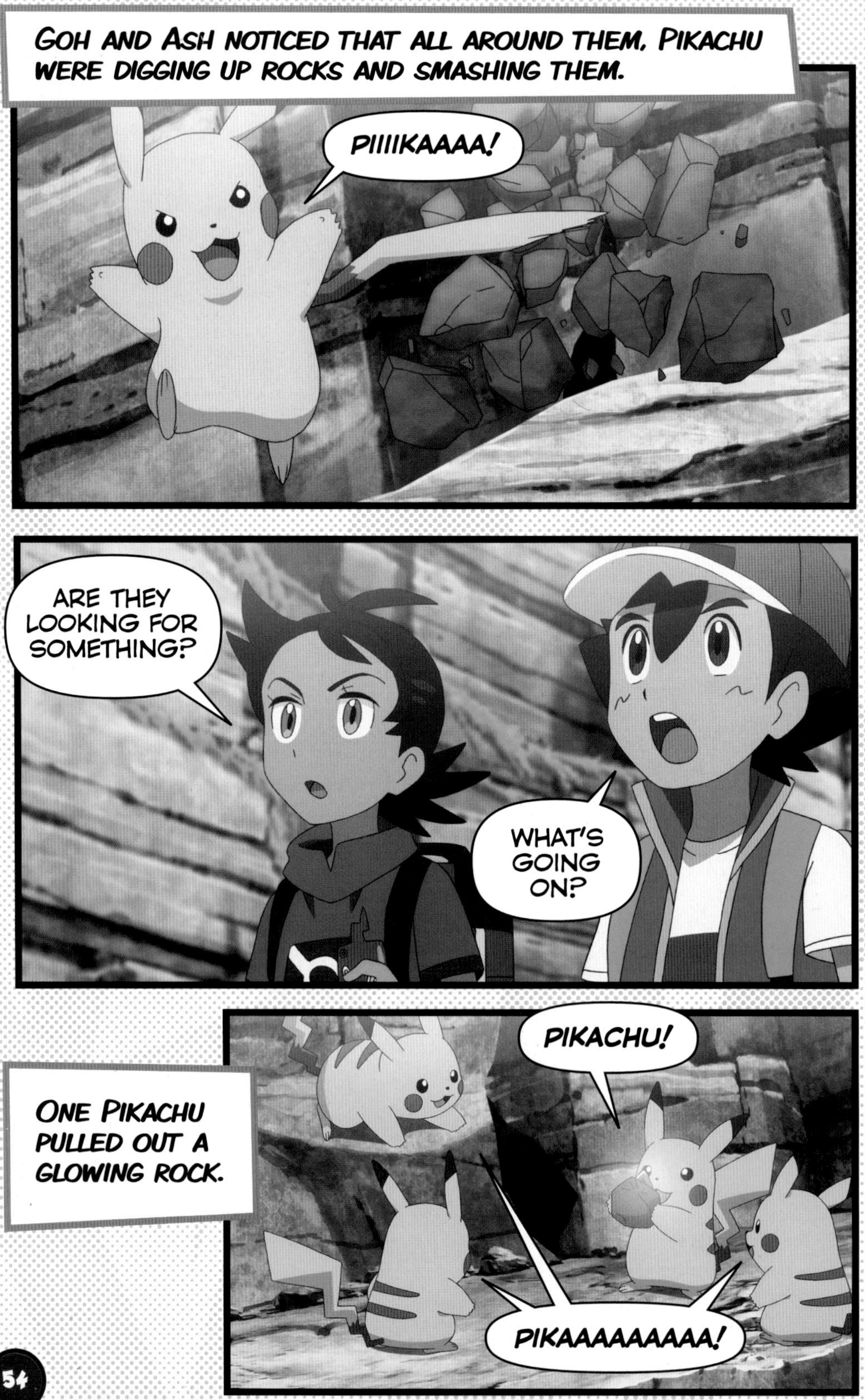
GOH AND ASH NOTICED THAT ALL AROUND THEM, PIKACHU WERE DIGGING UP ROCKS AND SMASHING THEM.
PIIIIKAAAA!
ARE THEY LOOKING FOR SOMETHING?
WHAT'S GOING ON?
ONE PIKACHU PULLED OUT A GLOWING ROCK.
PIKACHU!
PIKAAAAAAAAAA!

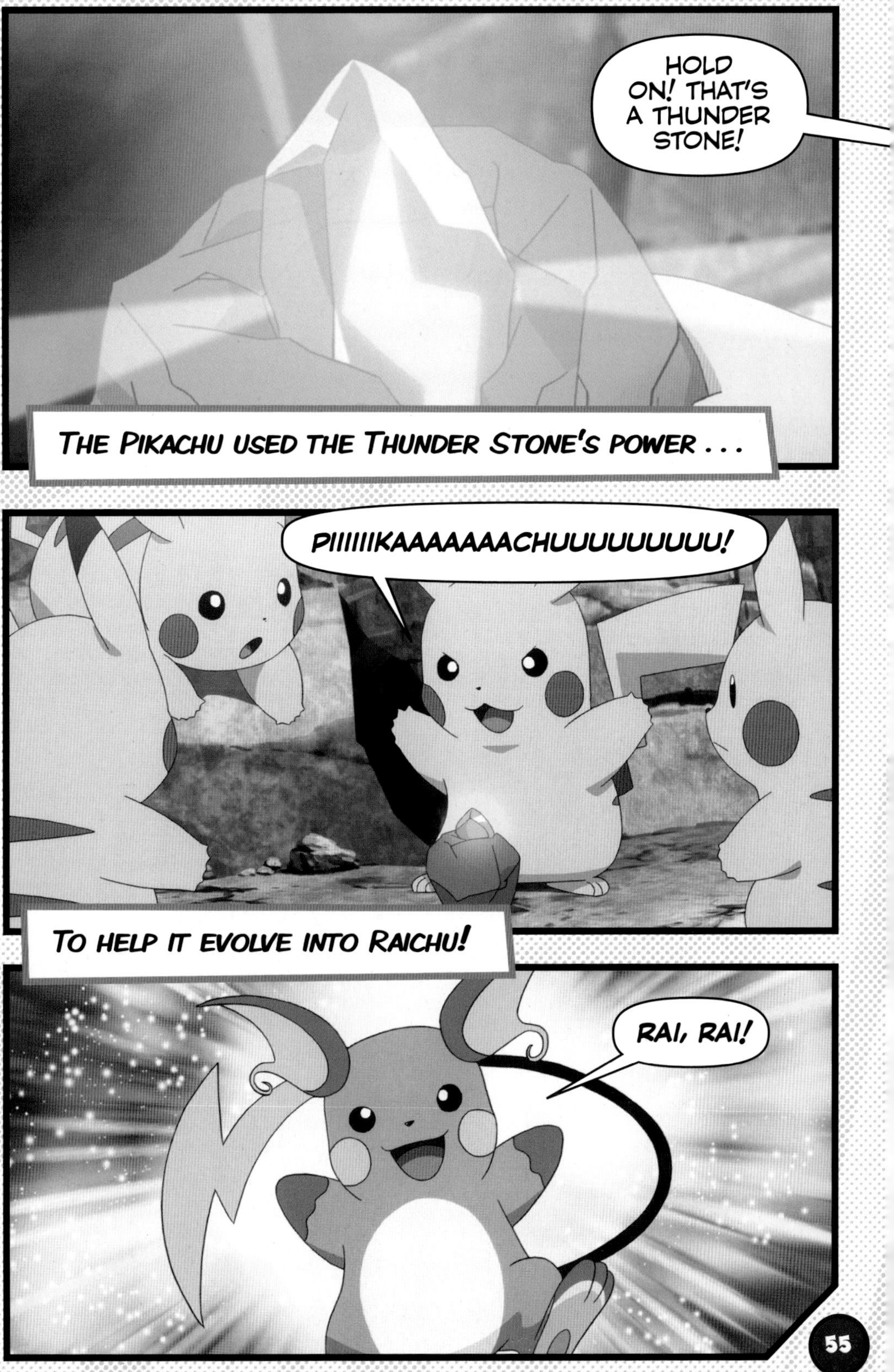
HOLD ON! THAT'S A THUNDER STONE!
THE PIKACHU USED THE THUNDER STONE'S POWER . . .
PIIIIIKAAAAAAACHUUUUUUUUU!
TO HELP IT EVOLVE INTO RAICHU!
RAI, RAI!

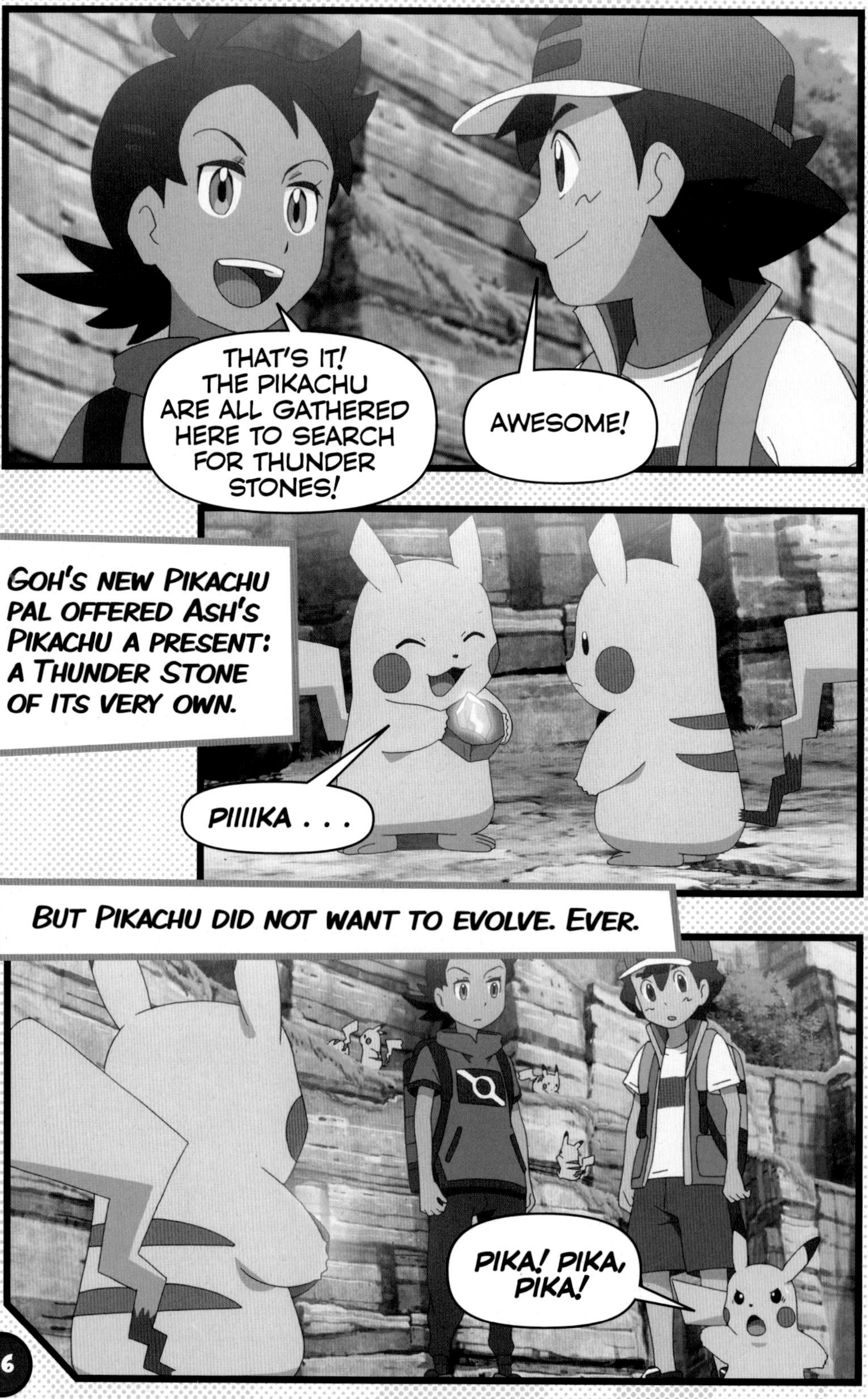
THAT'S IT! THE PIKACHU ARE ALL GATHERED HERE TO SEARCH FOR THUNDER STONES!
AWESOME!
GOH'S NEW PIKACHU PAL OFFERED ASH'S PIKACHU A PRESENT: A THUNDER STONE OF ITS VERY OWN.
PIIIKA . . .
BUT PIKACHU DID NOT WANT TO EVOLVE. EVER.
PIKA! PIKA, PIKA!

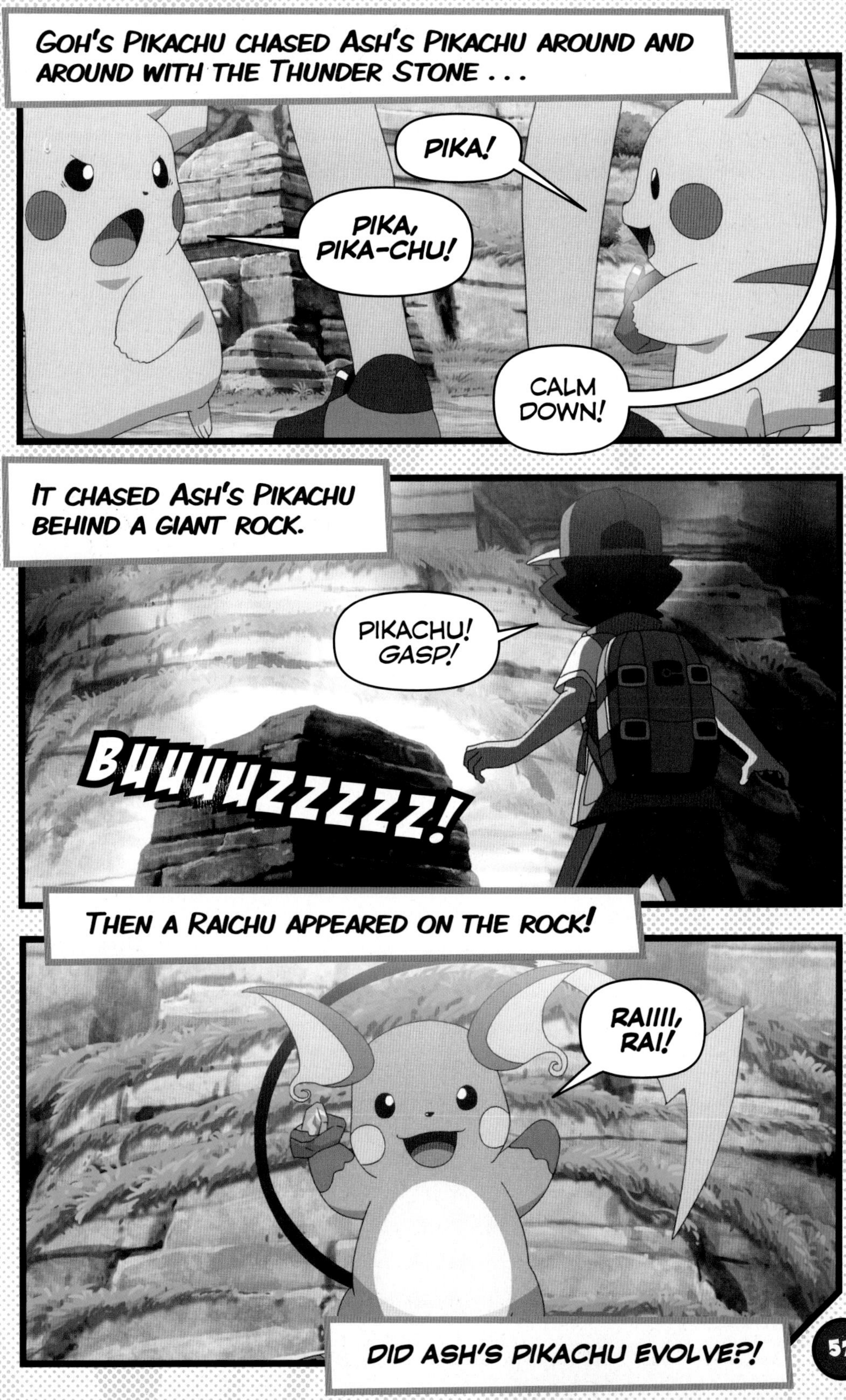
GOH'S PIKACHU CHASED ASH'S PIKACHU AROUND AND AROUND WITH THE THUNDER STONE . . .
PIKA!
PIKA, PIKA-CHU!
CALM DOWN!
IT CHASED ASH'S PIKACHU BEHIND A GIANT ROCK.
PIKACHU! GASP!
BUUUUZZZZZZ!
THEN A RAICHU APPEARED ON THE ROCK!
RAIIII, RAI!
DID ASH'S PIKACHU EVOLVE?!

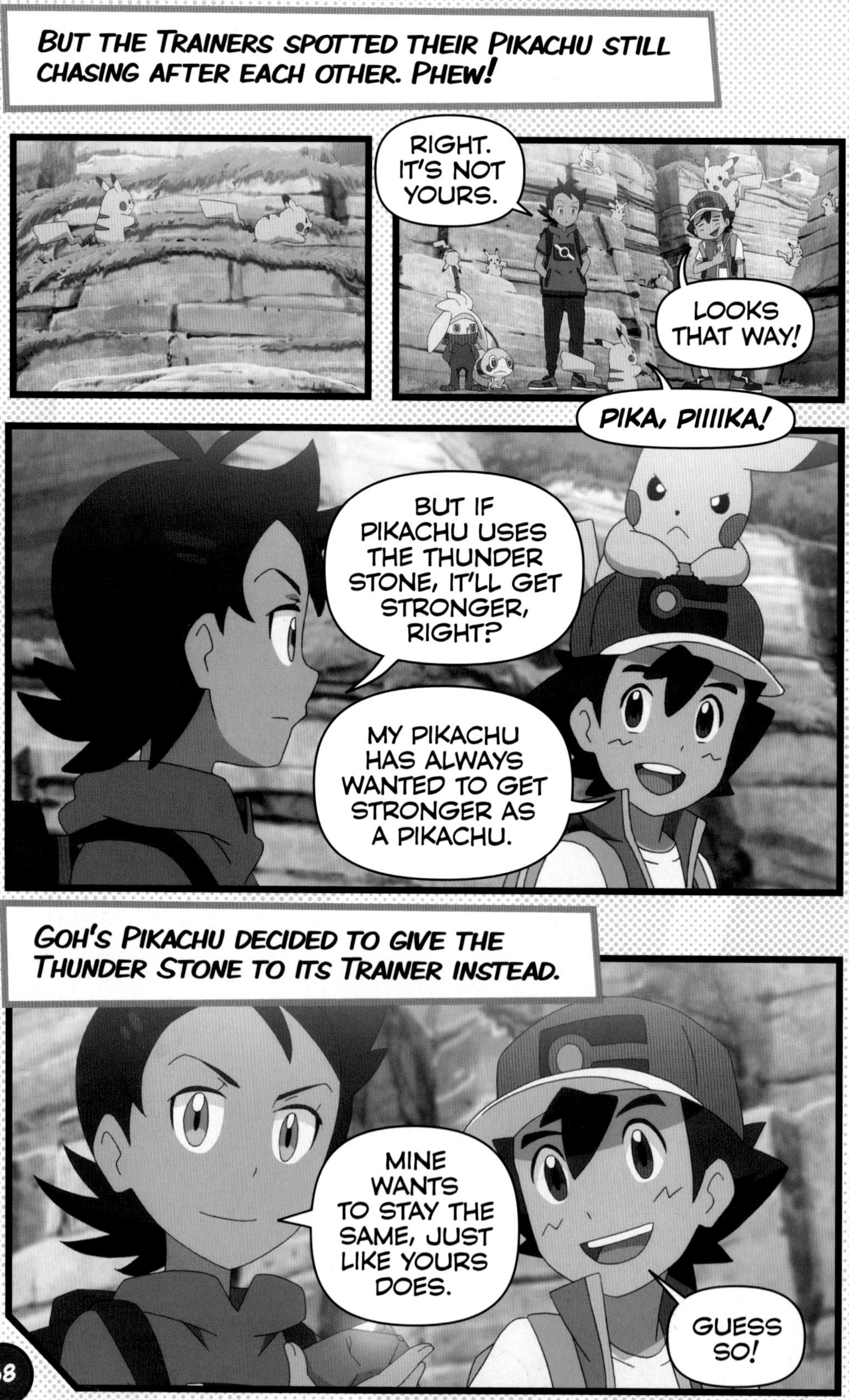
BUT THE TRAINERS SPOTTED THEIR PIKACHU STILL CHASING AFTER EACH OTHER. PHEW!
RIGHT. IT'S NOT YOURS.
LOOKS THAT WAY!
PIKA, PIIIIKA!
BUT IF PIKACHU USES THE THUNDER STONE, IT'LL GET STRONGER, RIGHT?
MY PIKACHU HAS ALWAYS WANTED TO GET STRONGER AS A PIKACHU.
GOH'S PIKACHU DECIDED TO GIVE THE THUNDER STONE TO ITS TRAINER INSTEAD.
MINE WANTS TO STAY THE SAME, JUST LIKE YOURS DOES.
GUESS SO!

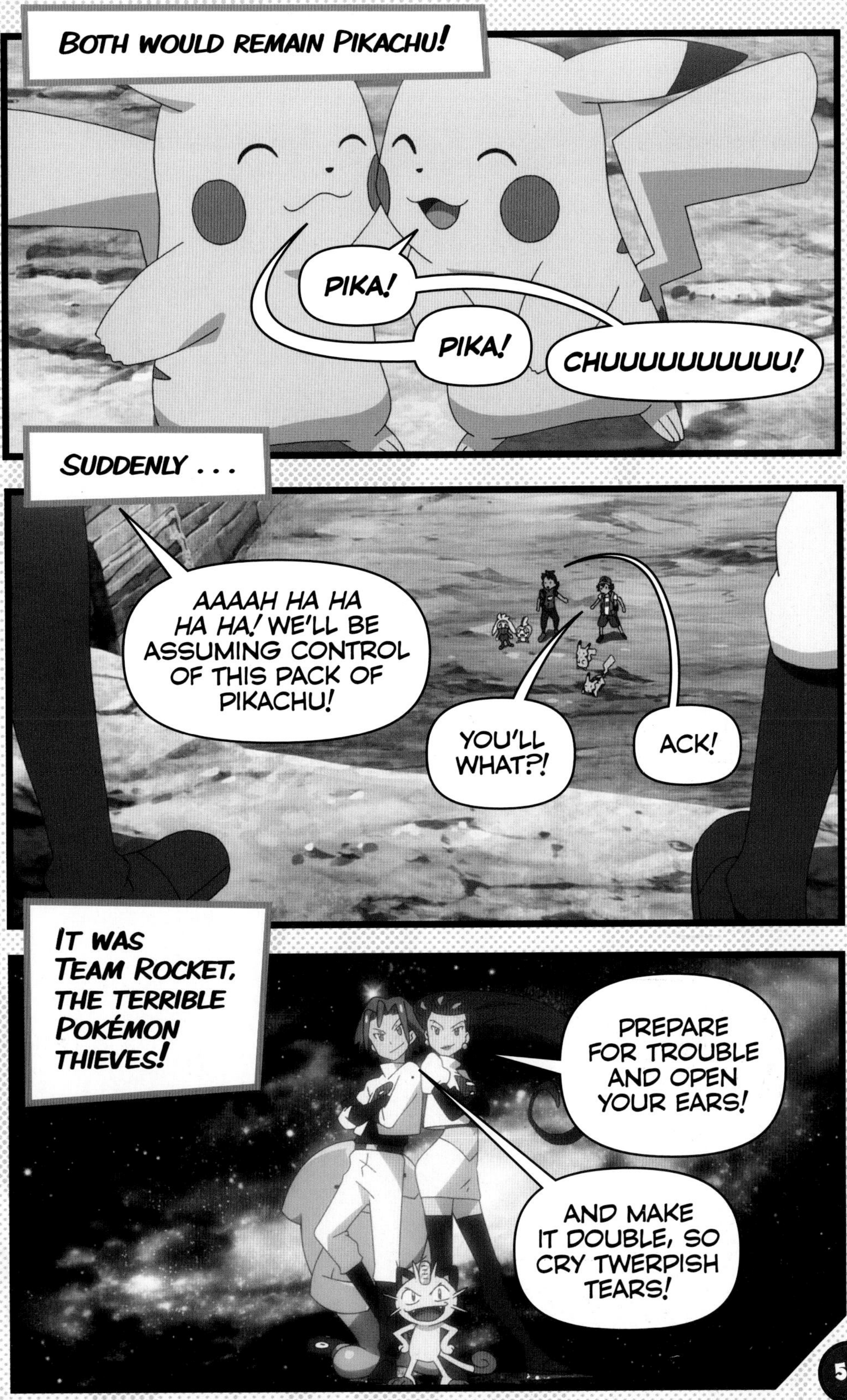
BOTH WOULD REMAIN PIKACHU!
PIKA!
PIKA!
CHUUUUUUUUUU!
SUDDENLY . . .
AAAAH HA HA HA HA! WE'LL BE ASSUMING CONTROL OF THIS PACK OF PIKACHU!
YOU'LL WHAT?!
ACK!
IT WAS TEAM ROCKET, THE TERRIBLE POKÉMON THIEVES!
PREPARE FOR TROUBLE AND OPEN YOUR EARS!
AND MAKE IT DOUBLE, SO CRY TWERPISH TEARS!

GOH'S PIKACHU CLIMBED FEARLESSLY UP TO TEAM ROCKET.
WOULD IT SHOCK THEM WITH A THUNDERBOLT OR BLAST THEM
OFF WITH AN IRON TAIL?

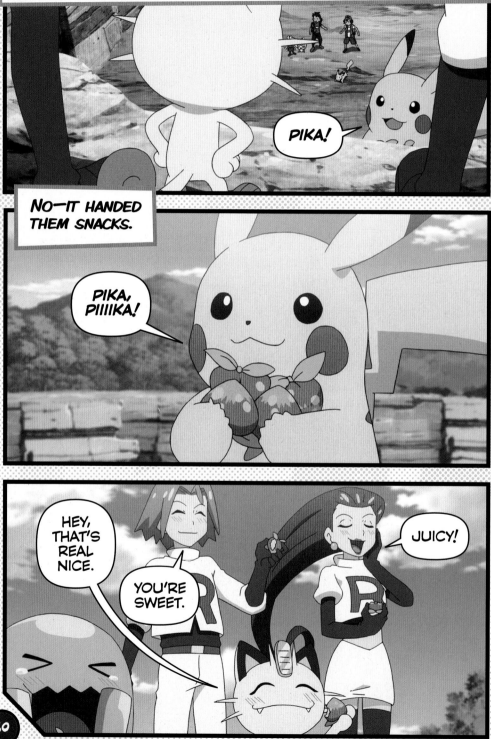

PIKA!

NO—IT HANDED THEM SNACKS.

PIKA, PIIIIKA!

HEY, THAT'S REAL NICE.

YOU'RE SWEET.

JUICY!

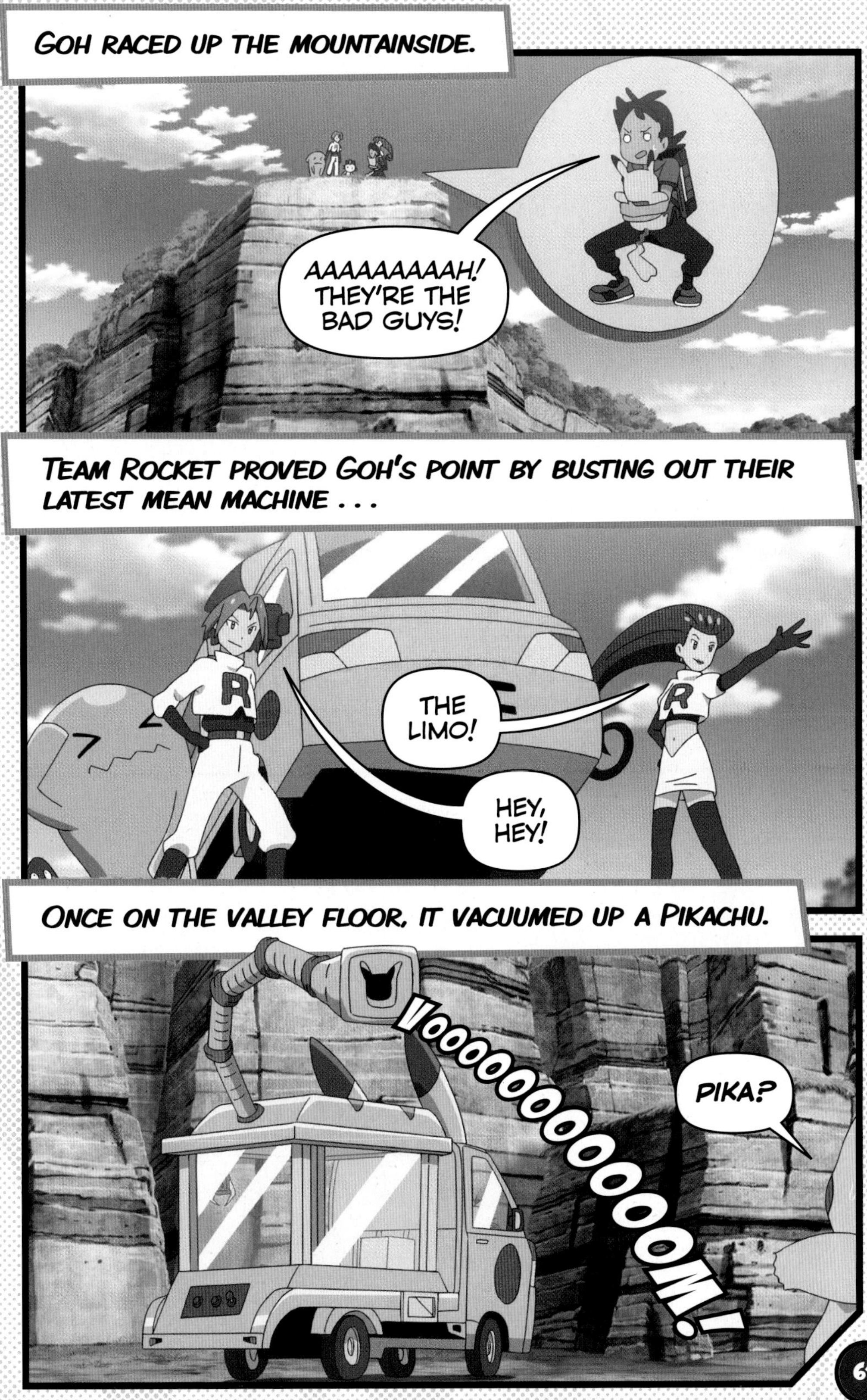
GOH RACED UP THE MOUNTAINSIDE.
AAAAAAAAAAH! THEY'RE THE BAD GUYS!
TEAM ROCKET PROVED GOH'S POINT BY BUSTING OUT THEIR LATEST MEAN MACHINE . . .
THE LIMO!
HEY, HEY!
ONCE ON THE VALLEY FLOOR, IT VACUUMED UP A PIKACHU.
VOOOOOOOOOOOOOM!
PIKA?

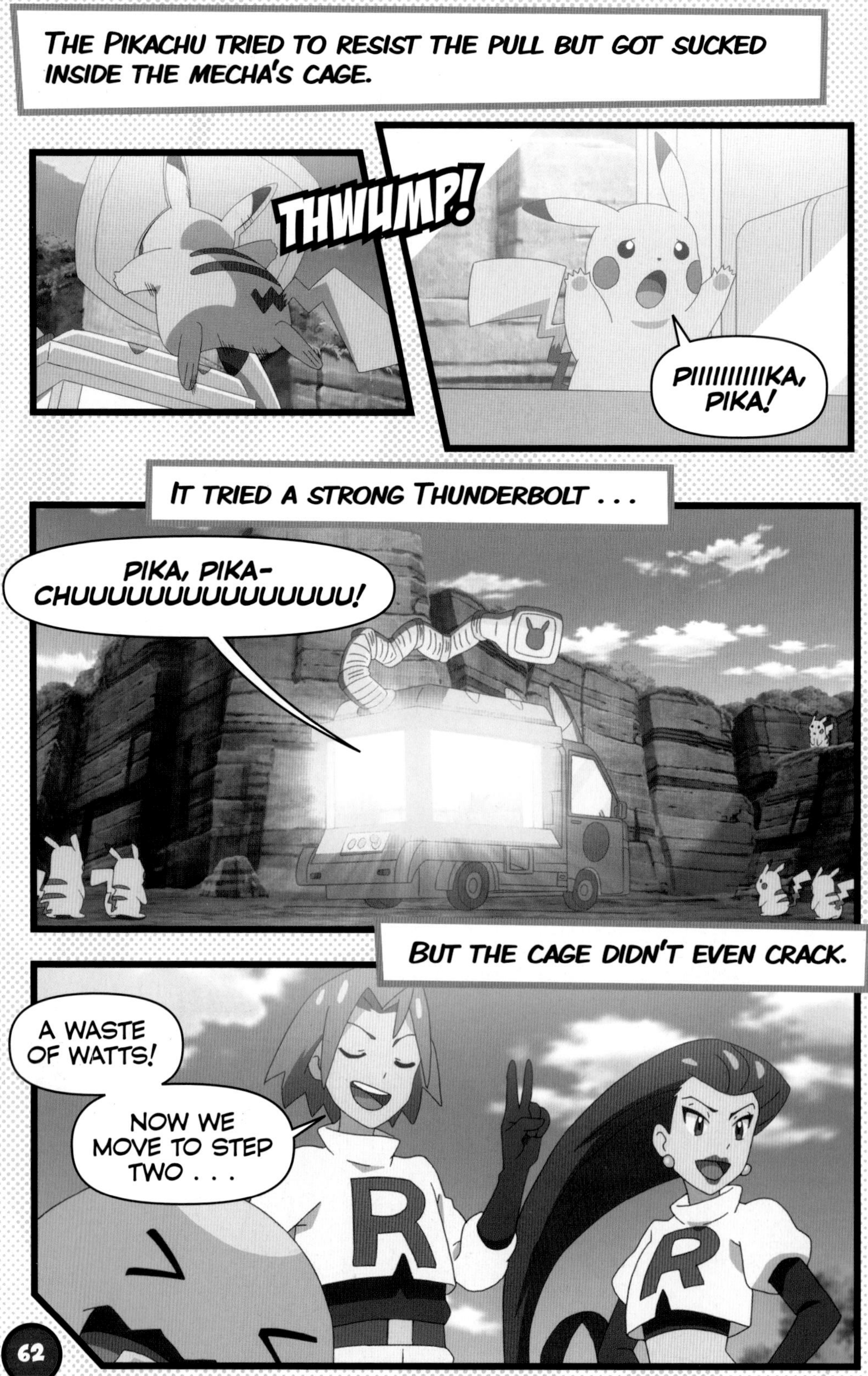
THE PIKACHU TRIED TO RESIST THE PULL BUT GOT SUCKED INSIDE THE MECHA'S CAGE.
THWUMP!
PIIIIIIIIIIKA, PIKA!
IT TRIED A STRONG THUNDERBOLT . . .
PIKA, PIKA-CHUUUUUUUUUUUUUU!
BUT THE CAGE DIDN'T EVEN CRACK.
A WASTE OF WATTS!
NOW WE MOVE TO STEP TWO . . .

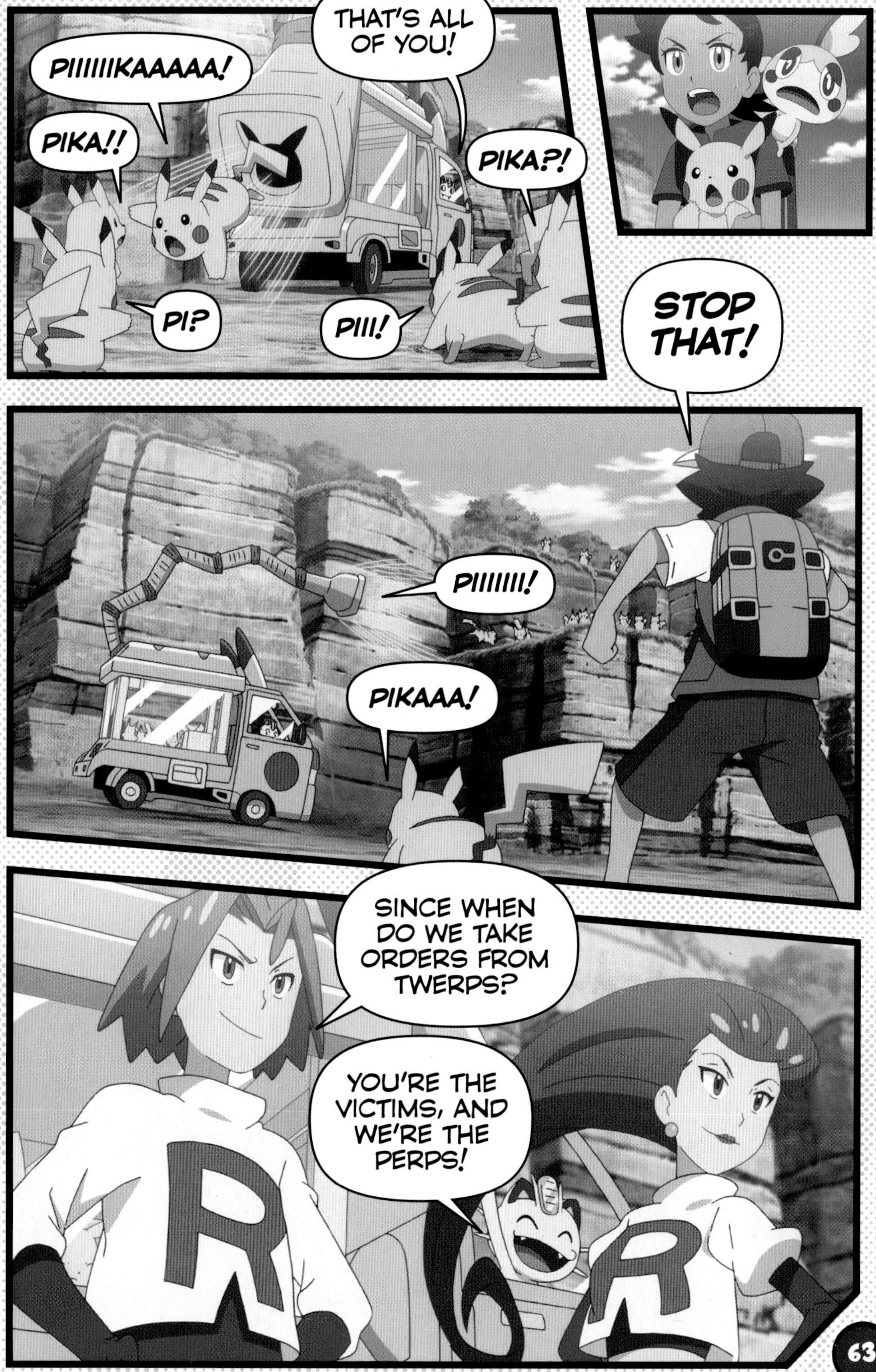
PIIIIIKAAAAA!
PIKA!!
THAT'S ALL OF YOU!
PIKA?!
PI?
PIII!
STOP THAT!
PIIIIIII!
PIKAAA!
SINCE WHEN DO WE TAKE ORDERS FROM TWERPS?
YOU'RE THE VICTIMS, AND WE'RE THE PERPS!

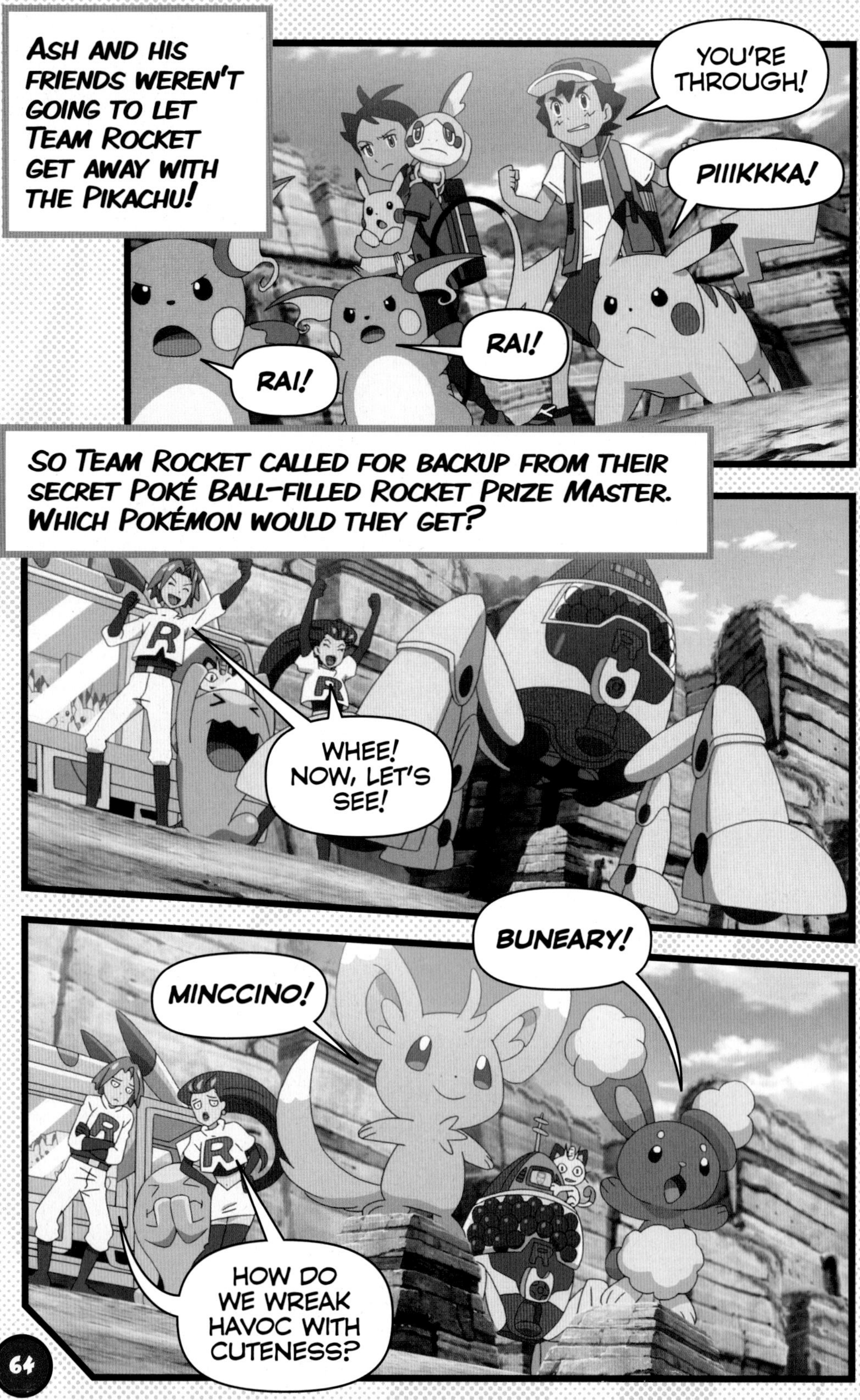
ASH AND HIS FRIENDS WEREN'T GOING TO LET TEAM ROCKET GET AWAY WITH THE PIKACHU!
YOU'RE THROUGH!
PIIIKKKA!
RAI!
RAI!
SO TEAM ROCKET CALLED FOR BACKUP FROM THEIR SECRET POKÉ BALL-FILLED ROCKET PRIZE MASTER. WHICH POKÉMON WOULD THEY GET?
WHEE! NOW, LET'S SEE!
MINCCINO!
BUNEARY!
HOW DO WE WREAK HAVOC WITH CUTENESS?

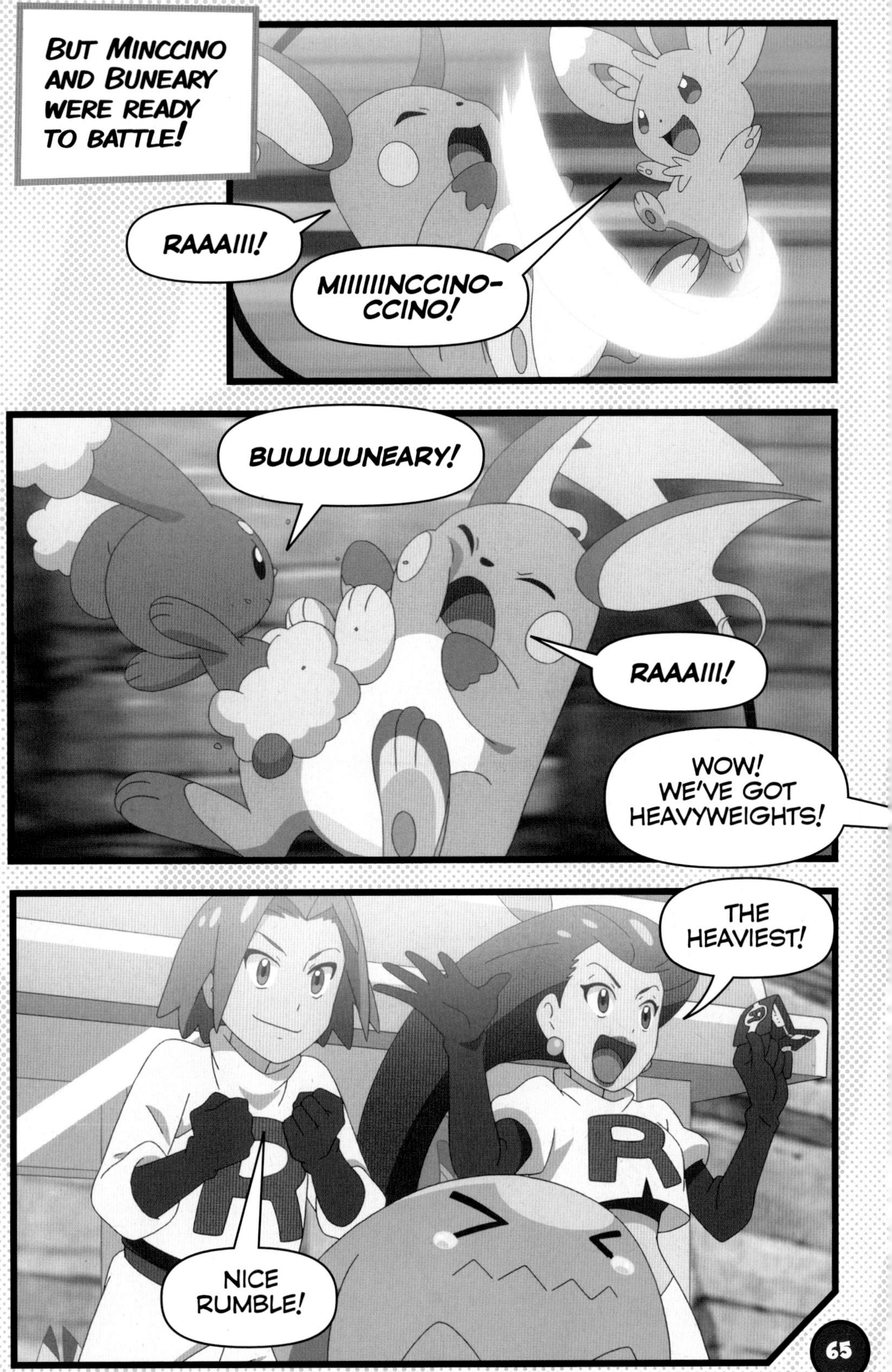

BUT MINCCINO AND BUNEARY WERE READY TO BATTLE!
RAAAIII!
MIIIIIINCCINO-CCINO!
BUUUUUNEARY!
RAAAIII!
WOW! WE'VE GOT HEAVYWEIGHTS!
THE HEAVIEST!
NICE RUMBLE!

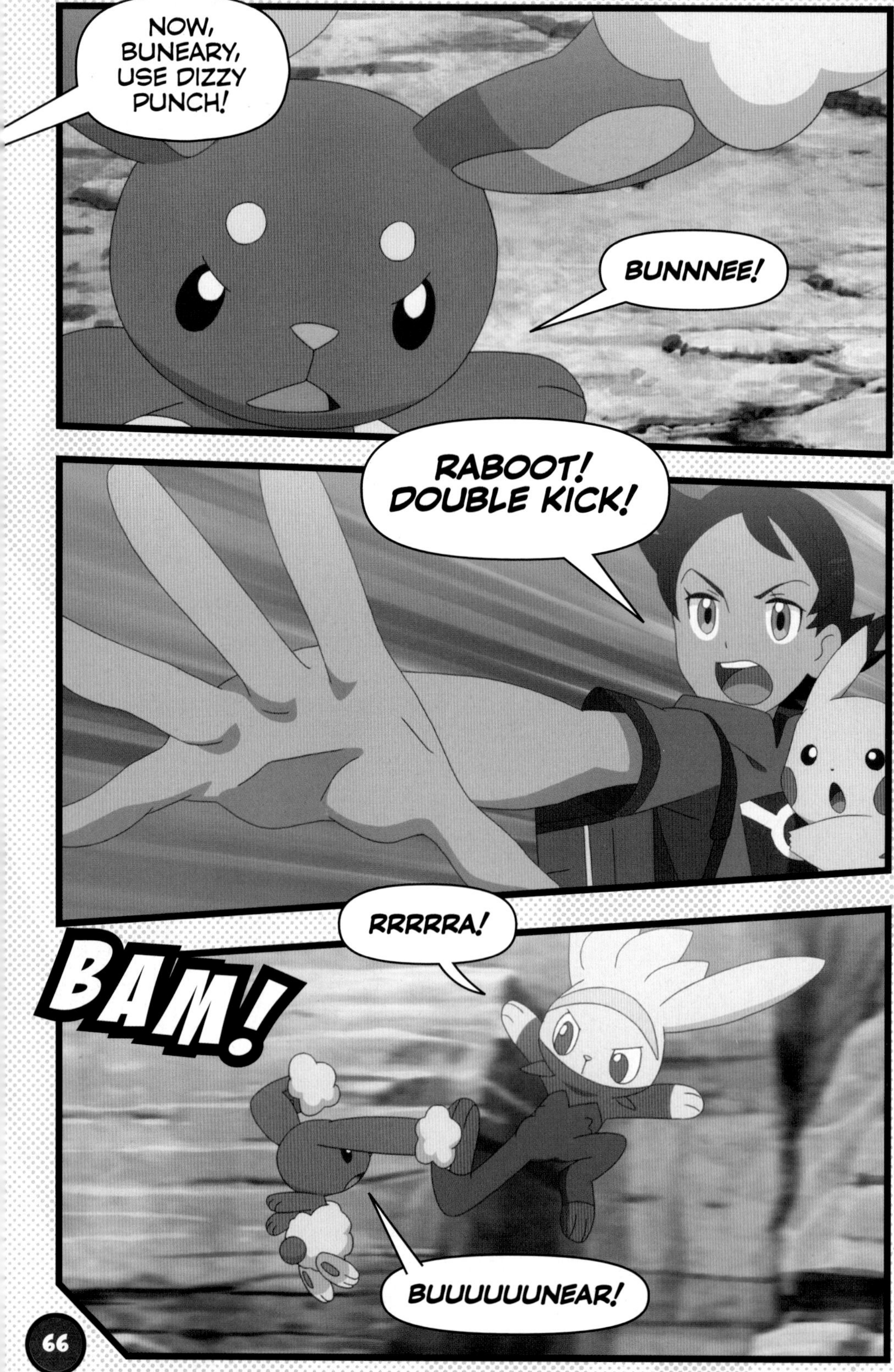
NOW, BUNEARY, USE DIZZY PUNCH!
BUNNNEE!
RABOOT! DOUBLE KICK!
RRRRRA!
BAM!
BUUUUUUNEAR!

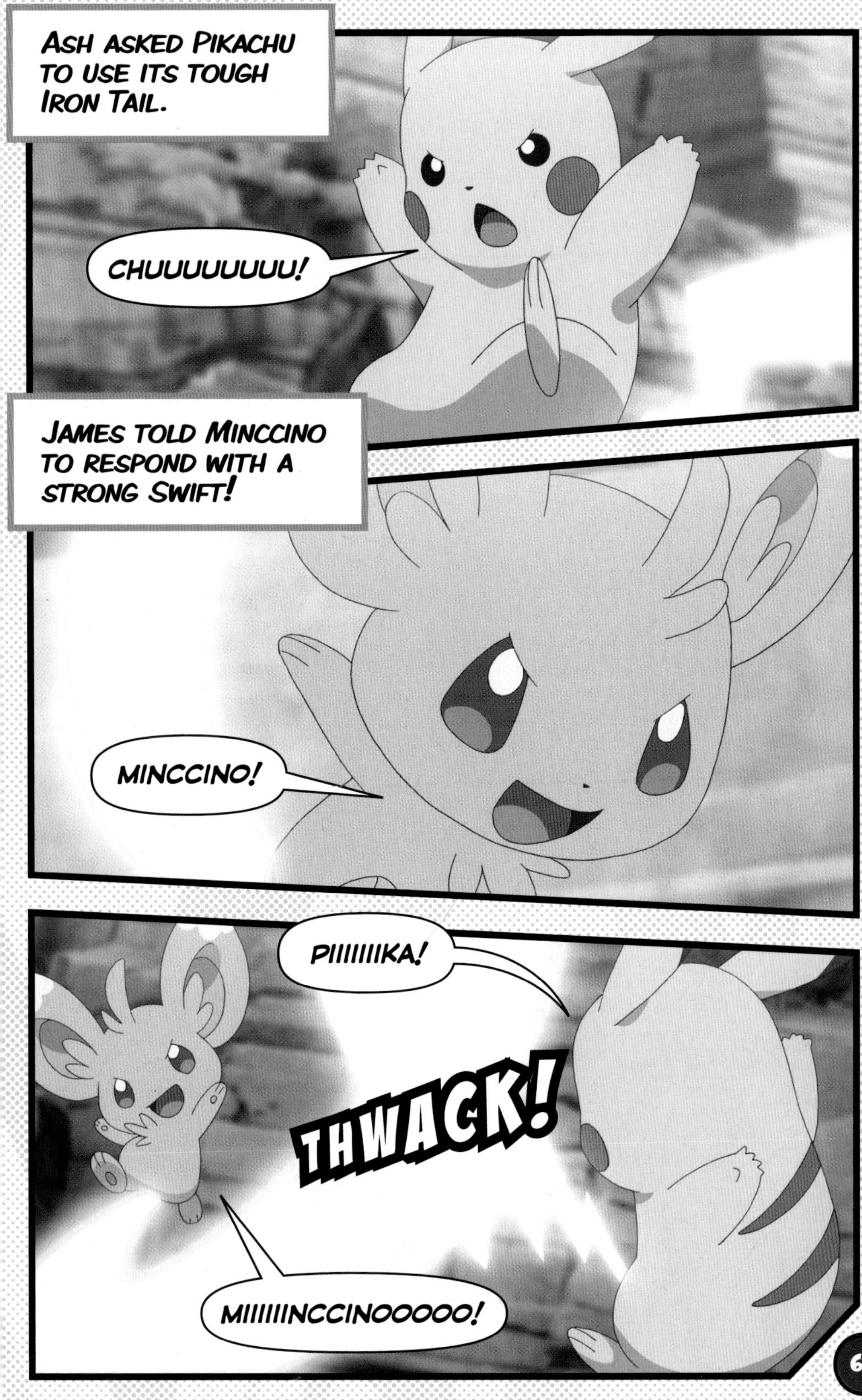
Ash asked Pikachu to use its tough Iron Tail.
CHUUUUUUUU!
James told Minccino to respond with a strong Swift!
MINCCINO!
PIIIIIIKA!
THWACK!
MIIIIIINCCINOOOOO!

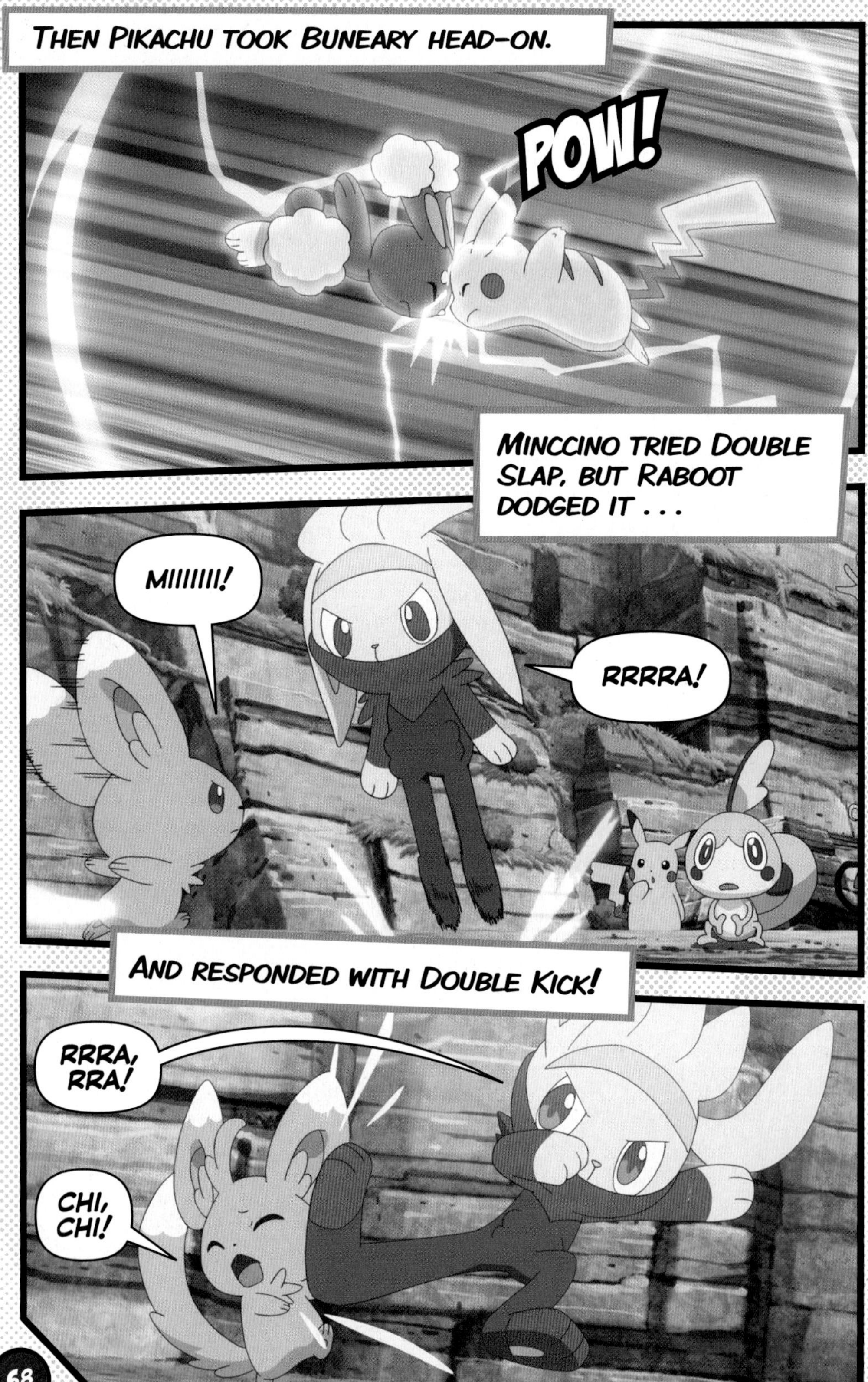
THEN PIKACHU TOOK BUNEARY HEAD-ON.
POW!
MINCCINO TRIED DOUBLE SLAP, BUT RABOOT DODGED IT . . .
MIIIIIII!
RRRRA!
AND RESPONDED WITH DOUBLE KICK!
RRRA, RRA!
CHI, CHI!

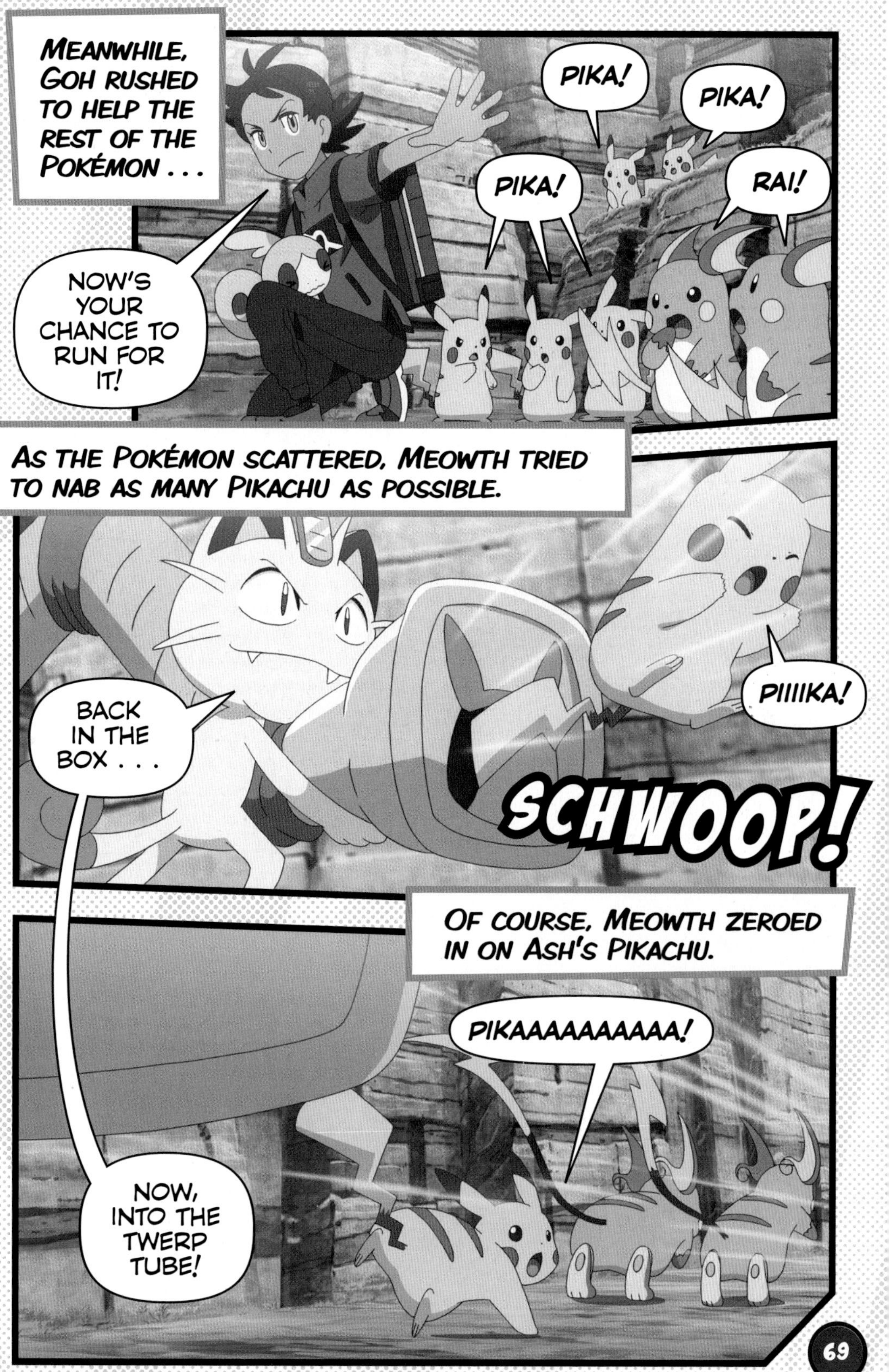
MEANWHILE, GOH RUSHED TO HELP THE REST OF THE POKÉMON . . .
NOW'S YOUR CHANCE TO RUN FOR IT!
PIKA!
PIKA!
PIKA!
RAI!
AS THE POKÉMON SCATTERED, MEOWTH TRIED TO NAB AS MANY PIKACHU AS POSSIBLE.
BACK IN THE BOX . . .
PIIIIKA!
SCHWOOP!
OF COURSE, MEOWTH ZEROED IN ON ASH'S PIKACHU.
PIKAAAAAAAAAA!
NOW, INTO THE TWERP TUBE!

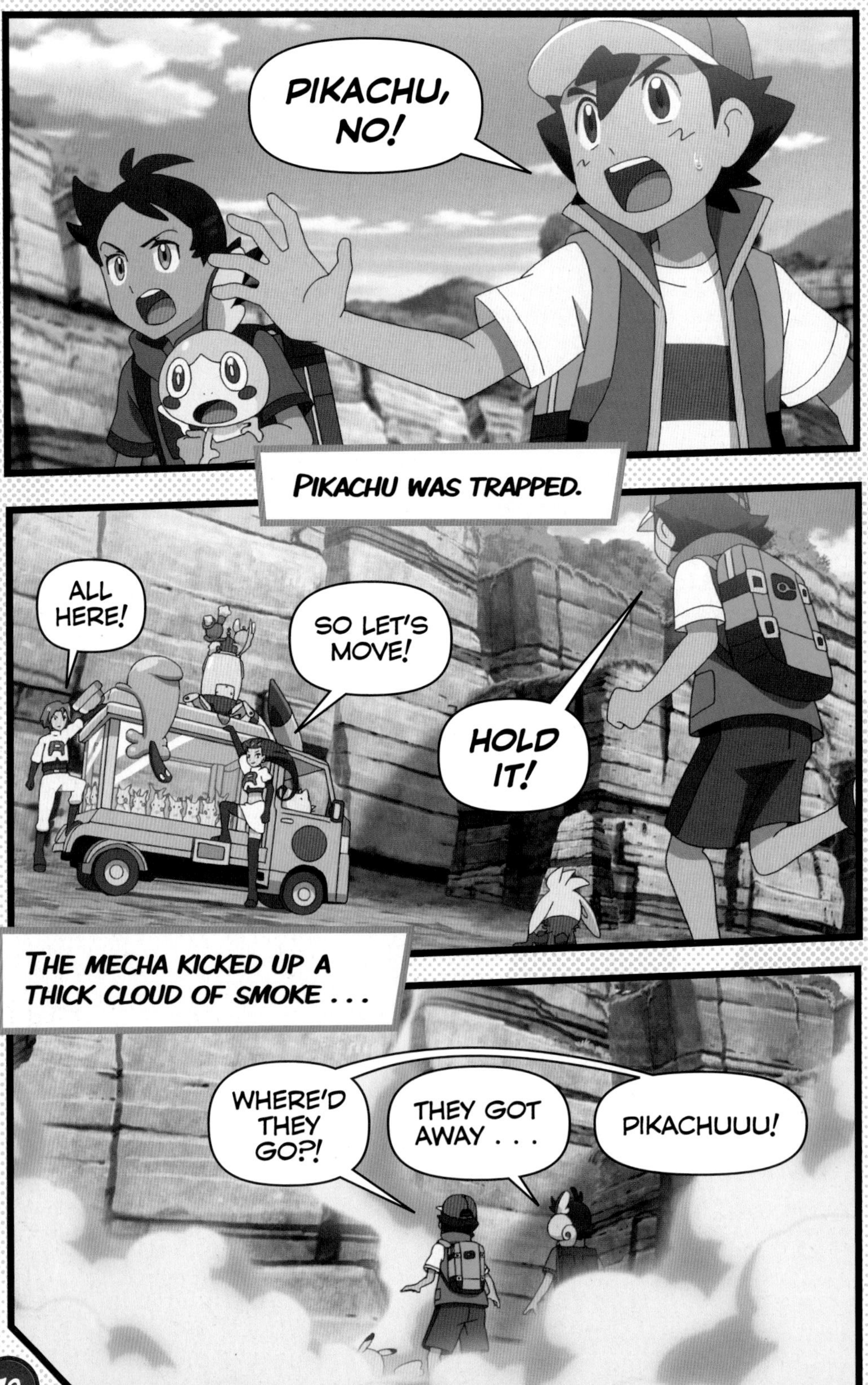
PIKACHU, NO!
PIKACHU WAS TRAPPED.
ALL HERE!
SO LET'S MOVE!
HOLD IT!
THE MECHA KICKED UP A THICK CLOUD OF SMOKE . . .
WHERE'D THEY GO?!
THEY GOT AWAY . . .
PIKACHUUU!

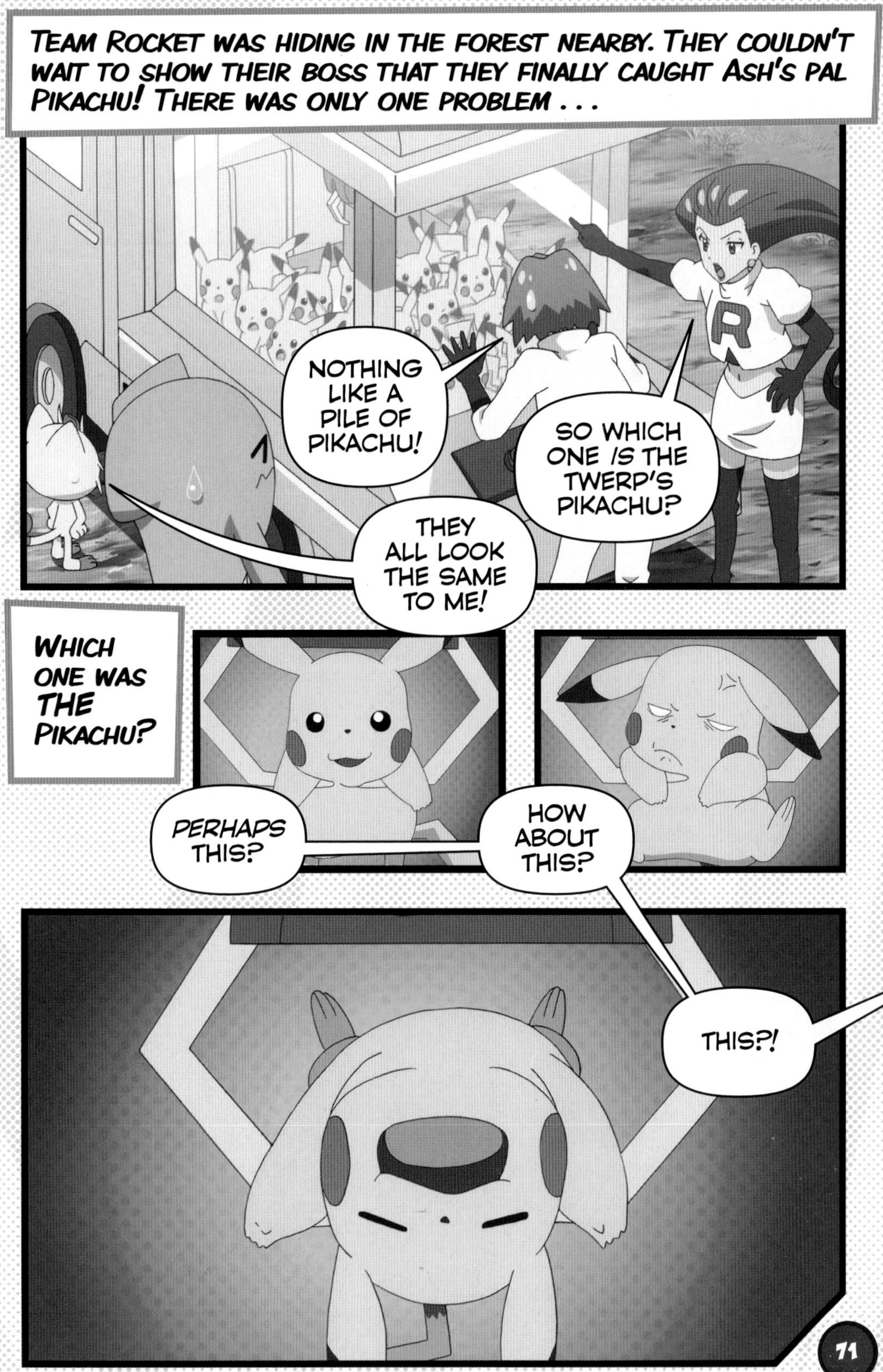
TEAM ROCKET WAS HIDING IN THE FOREST NEARBY. THEY COULDN'T WAIT TO SHOW THEIR BOSS THAT THEY FINALLY CAUGHT ASH'S PAL PIKACHU! THERE WAS ONLY ONE PROBLEM . . .
NOTHING LIKE A PILE OF PIKACHU!
SO WHICH ONE *IS* THE TWERP'S PIKACHU?
THEY ALL LOOK THE SAME TO ME!
WHICH ONE WAS *THE* PIKACHU?
*PERHAPS* THIS?
HOW ABOUT THIS?
THIS?!

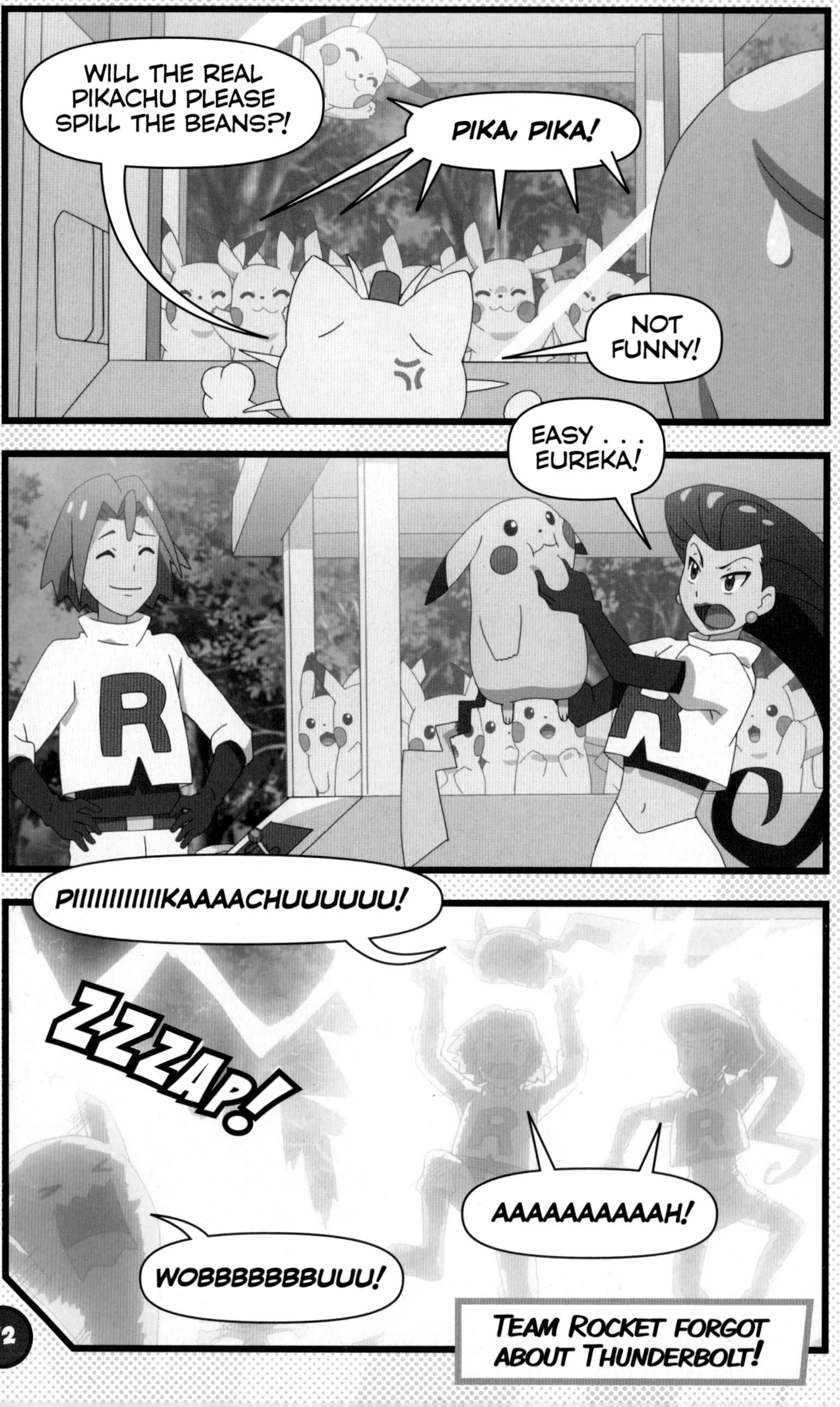
WILL THE REAL PIKACHU PLEASE SPILL THE BEANS?!
PIKA, PIKA!
NOT FUNNY!
EASY . . . EUREKA!
PIIIIIIIIIIIIKAAAACHUUUUUU!
ZZZAP!
AAAAAAAAAAH!
WOBBBBBBBUUU!
TEAM ROCKET FORGOT ABOUT THUNDERBOLT!

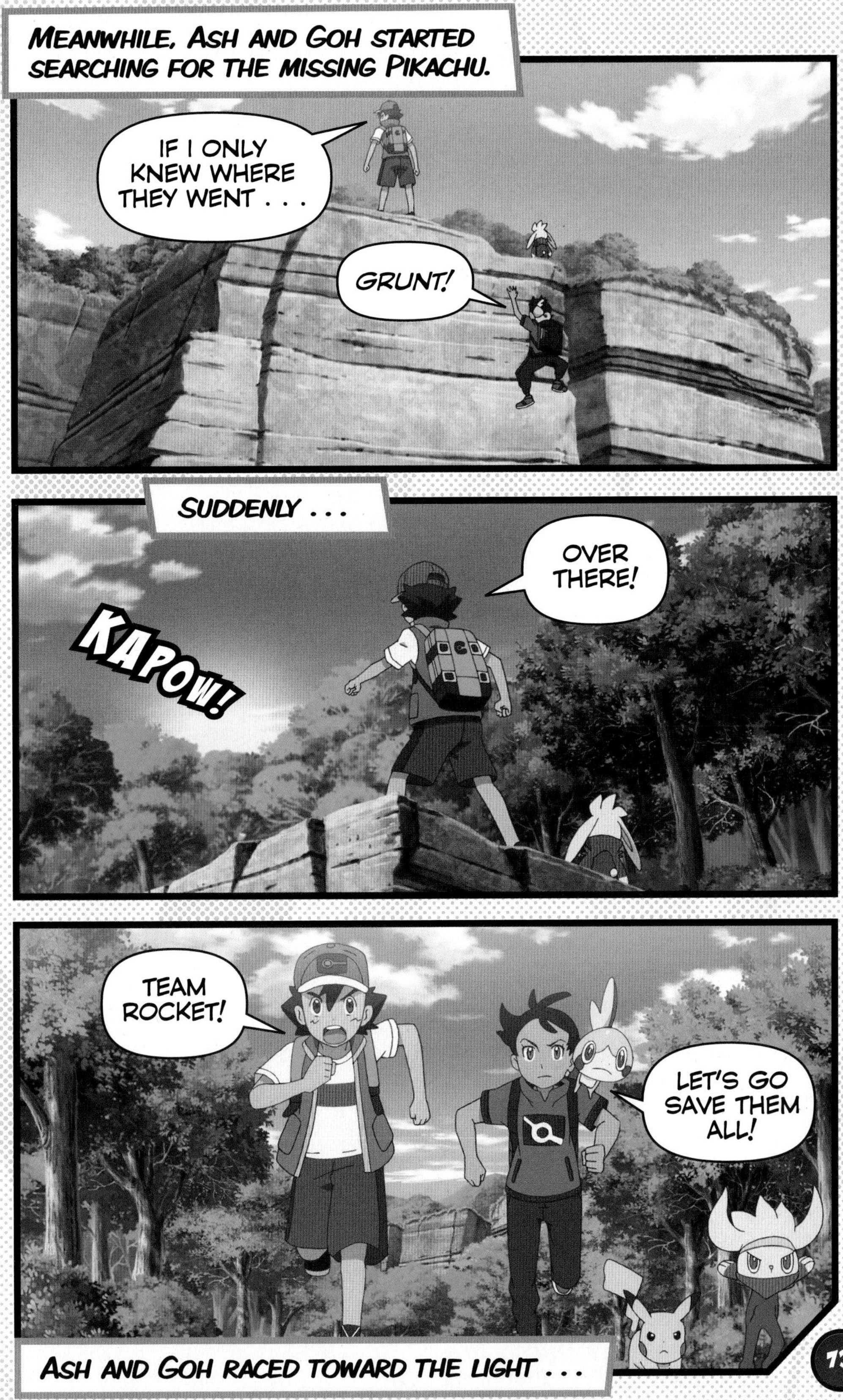
MEANWHILE, ASH AND GOH STARTED SEARCHING FOR THE MISSING PIKACHU.
IF I ONLY KNEW WHERE THEY WENT . . .
GRUNT!
SUDDENLY . . .
OVER THERE!
KAPOW!
TEAM ROCKET!
LET'S GO SAVE THEM ALL!
ASH AND GOH RACED TOWARD THE LIGHT . . .

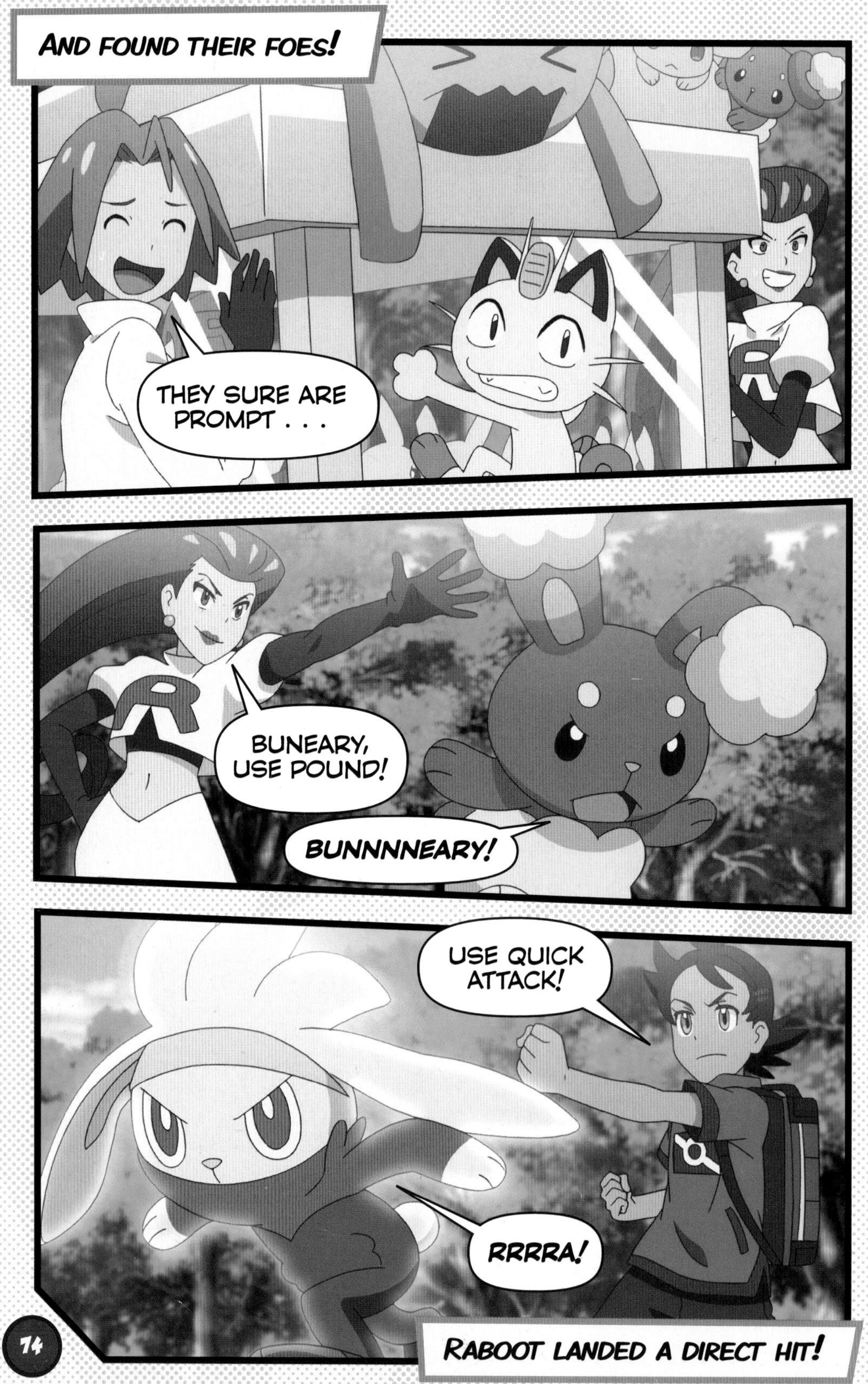
AND FOUND THEIR FOES!
THEY SURE ARE PROMPT . . .
BUNEARY, USE POUND!
BUNNNNEARY!
USE QUICK ATTACK!
RRRRA!
RABOOT LANDED A DIRECT HIT!

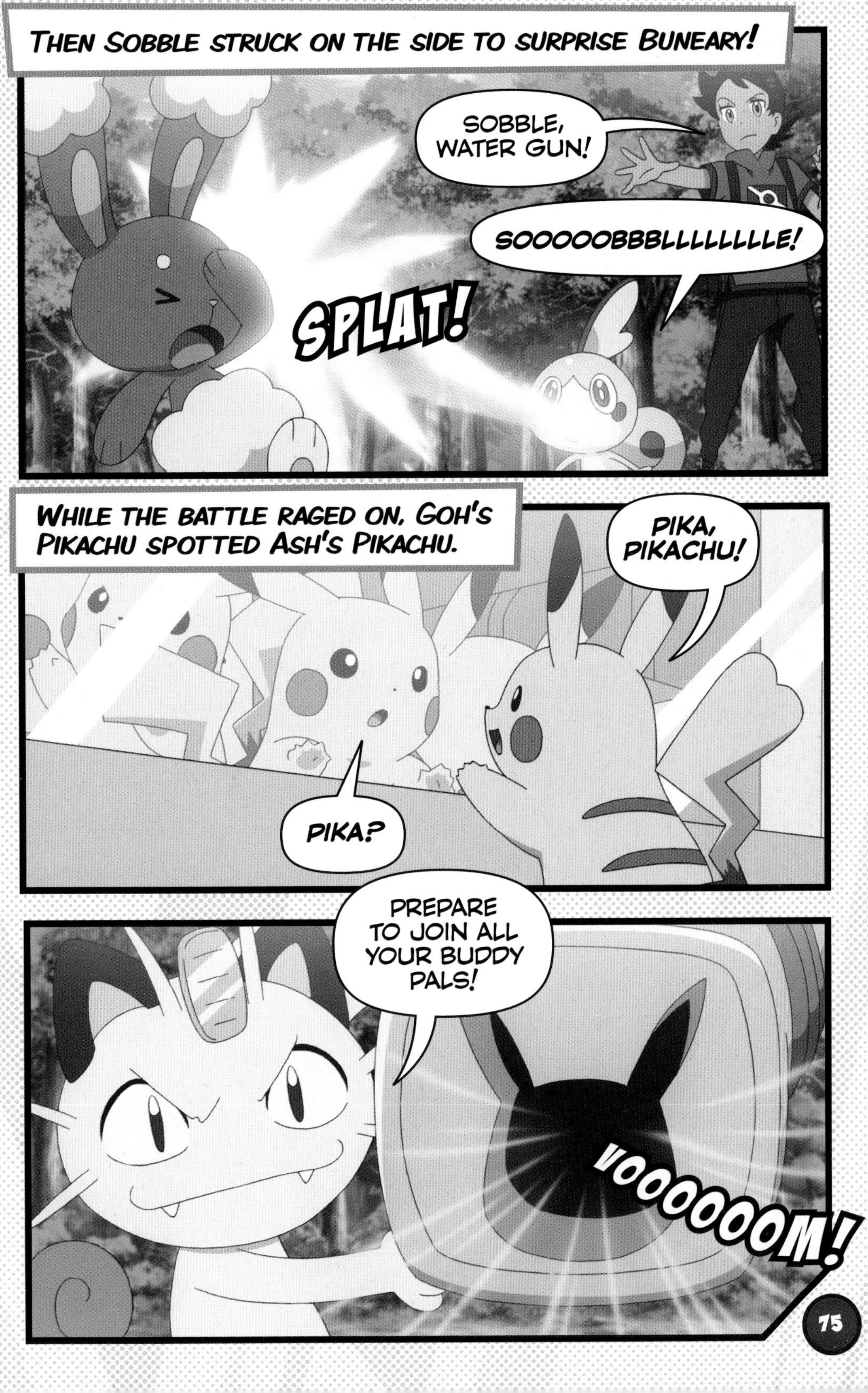
THEN SOBBLE STRUCK ON THE SIDE TO SURPRISE BUNEARY!
SOBBLE, WATER GUN!
SOOOOOBBBLLLLLLLLE!
SPLAT!
WHILE THE BATTLE RAGED ON, GOH'S PIKACHU SPOTTED ASH'S PIKACHU.
PIKA, PIKACHU!
PIKA?
PREPARE TO JOIN ALL YOUR BUDDY PALS!
VOOOOOOM!

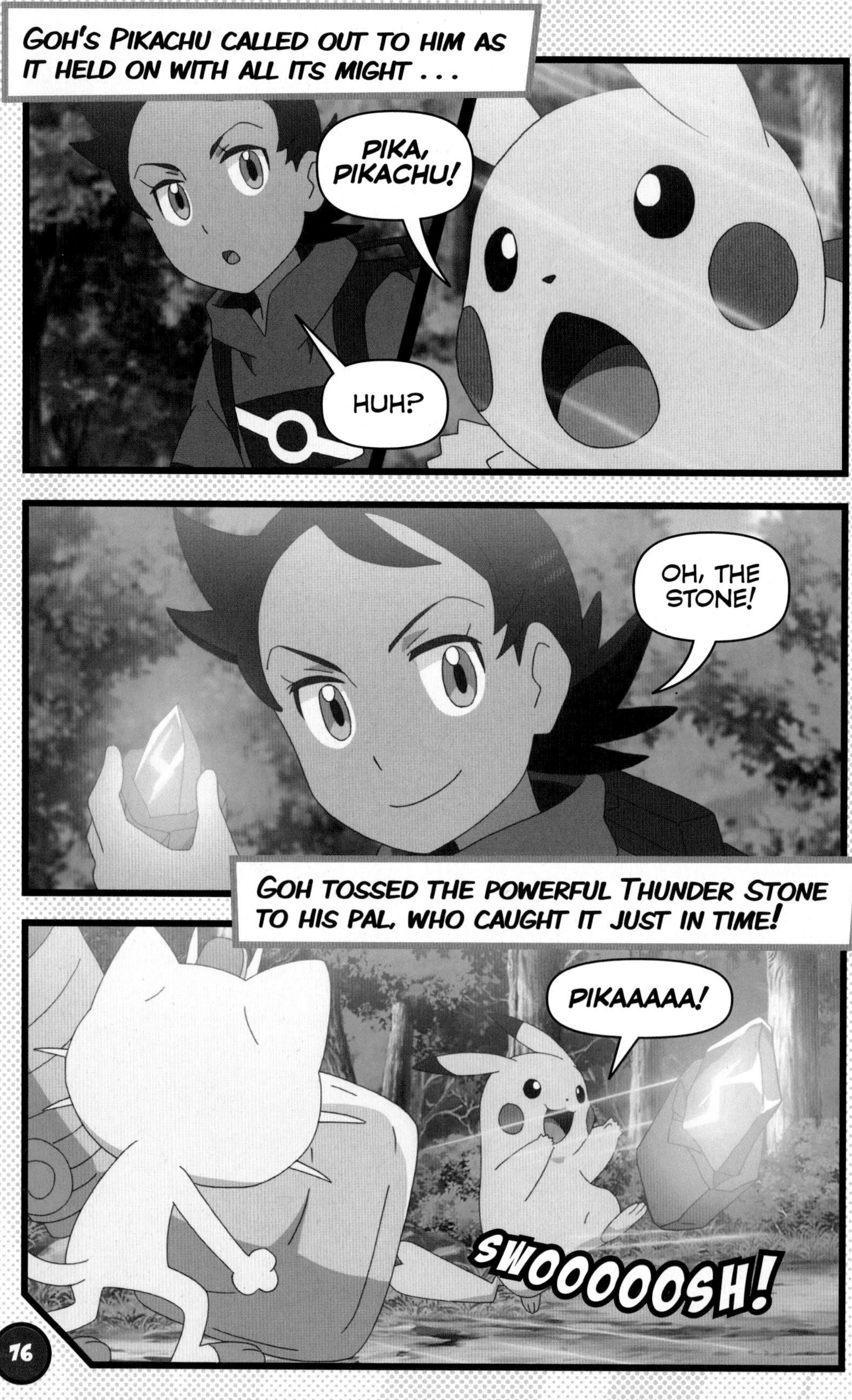

GOH'S PIKACHU CALLED OUT TO HIM AS IT HELD ON WITH ALL ITS MIGHT . . .
PIKA, PIKACHU!
HUH?
OH, THE STONE!
GOH TOSSED THE POWERFUL THUNDER STONE TO HIS PAL, WHO CAUGHT IT JUST IN TIME!
PIKAAAAA!
SWOOOOOOSH!

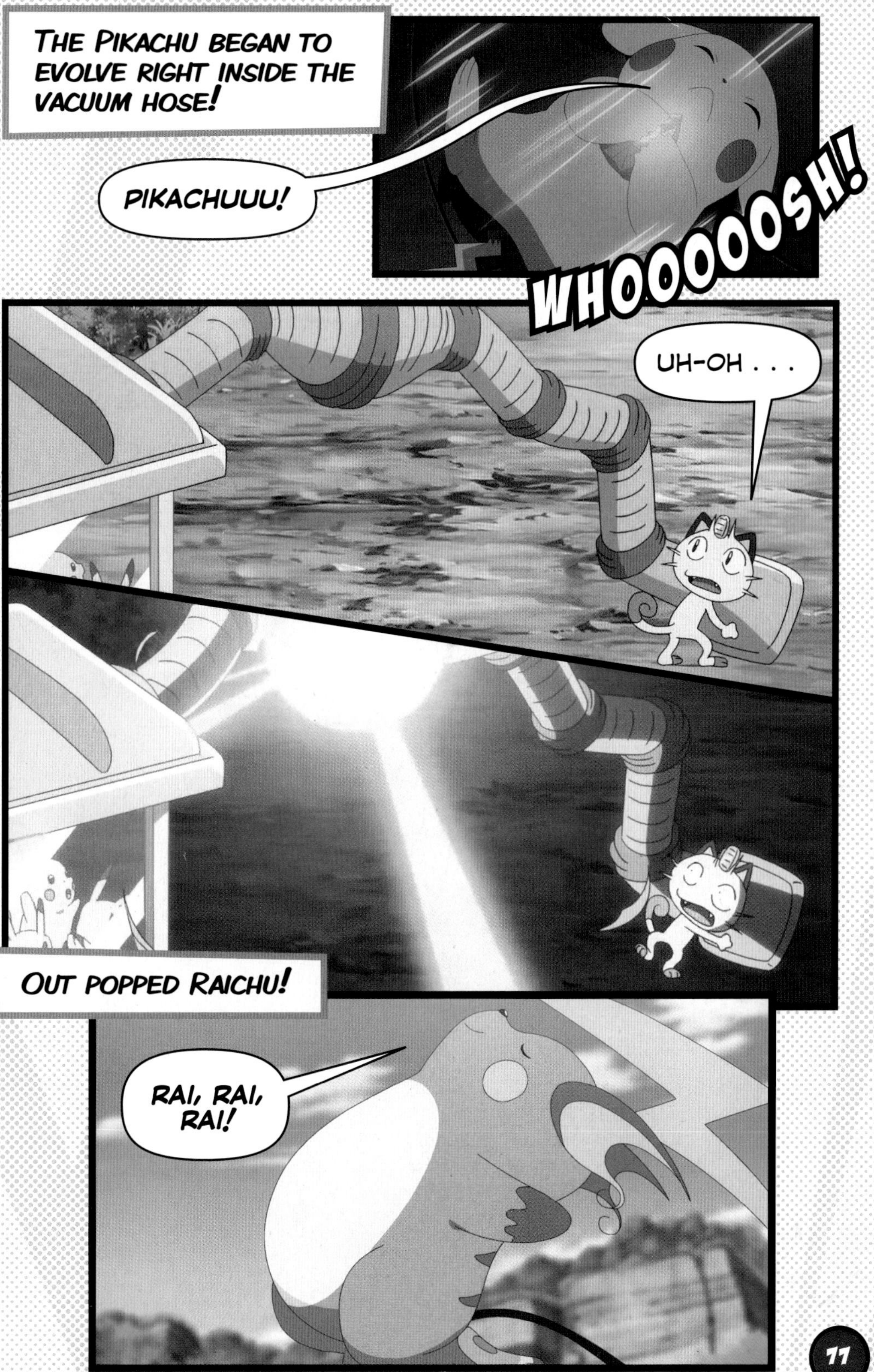
THE PIKACHU BEGAN TO EVOLVE RIGHT INSIDE THE VACUUM HOSE!
PIKACHUUU!
WHOOOOOOSH!
UH-OH . . .
OUT POPPED RAICHU!
RAI, RAI, RAI!

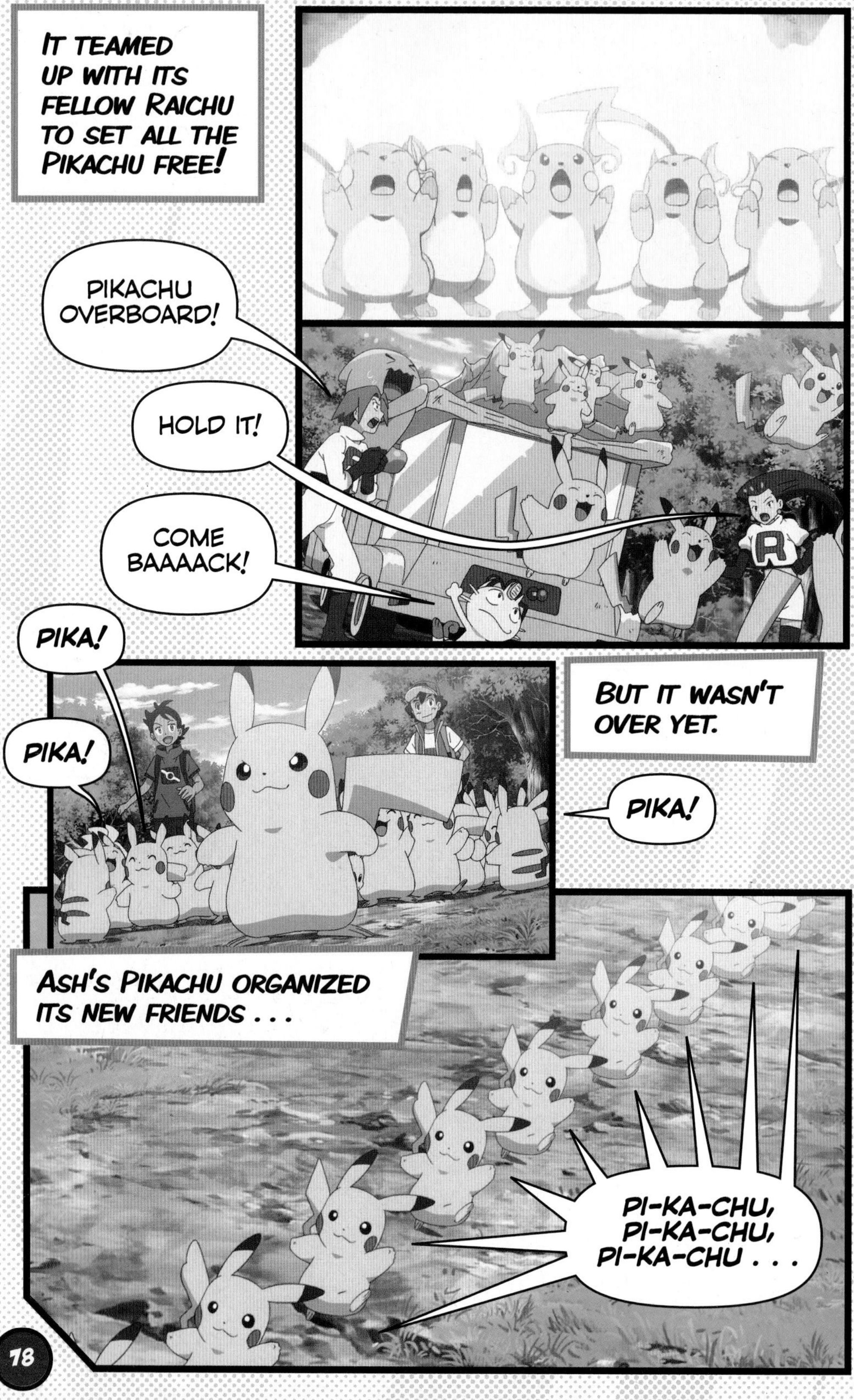
It teamed up with its fellow Raichu to set all the Pikachu free!
Pikachu overboard!
Hold it!
Come baaaack!
Pika!
Pika!
But it wasn't over yet.
Pika!
Ash's Pikachu organized its new friends . . .
Pi-ka-chu, pi-ka-chu, pi-ka-chu . . .

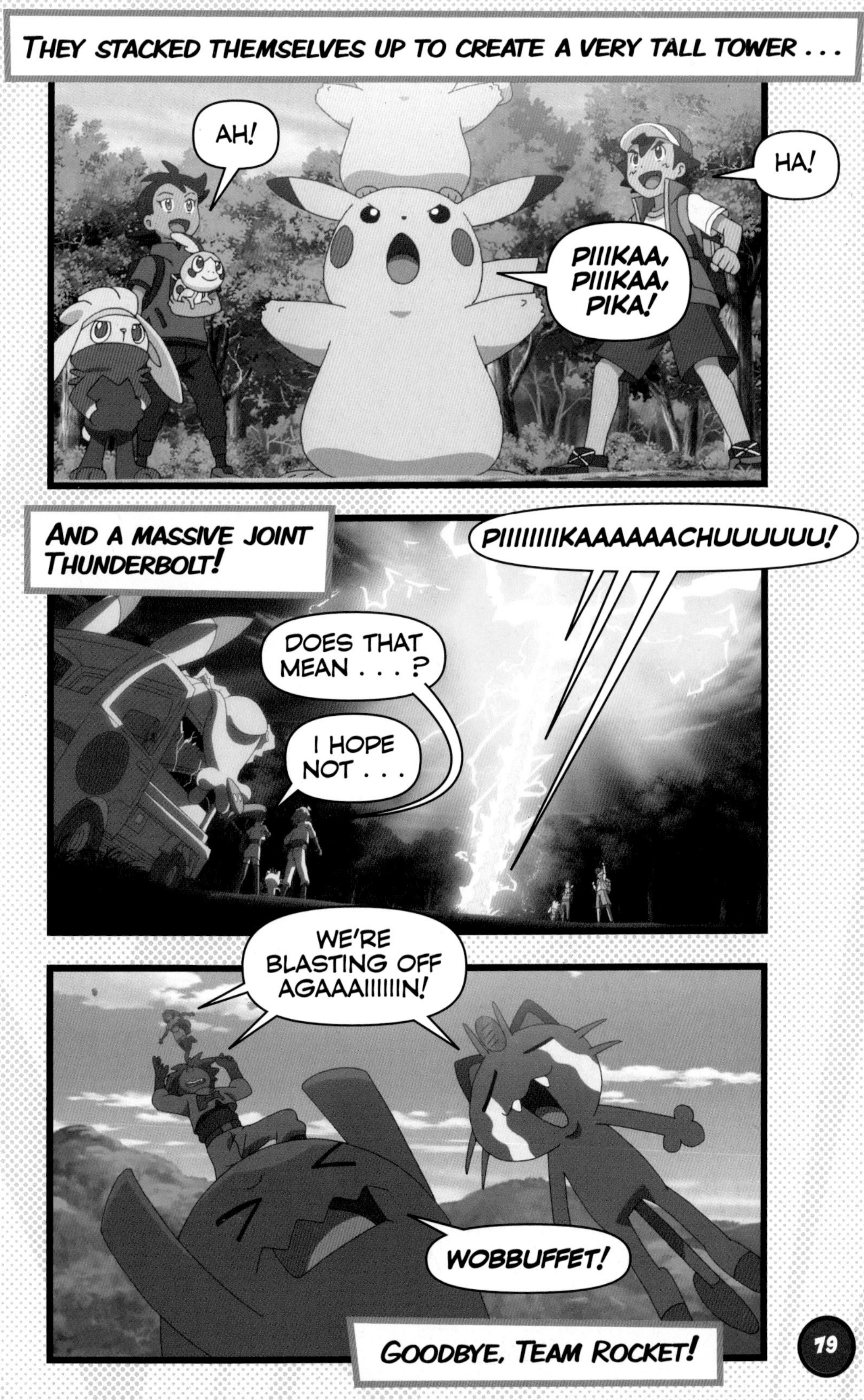
THEY STACKED THEMSELVES UP TO CREATE A VERY TALL TOWER . . .
AH!
HA!
PIIIKAA, PIIIKAA, PIKA!
AND A MASSIVE JOINT THUNDERBOLT!
PIIIIIIIIKAAAAAACHUUUUUU!
DOES THAT MEAN . . . ?
I HOPE NOT . . .
WE'RE BLASTING OFF AGAAAIIIIIIN!
WOBBUFFET!
GOODBYE, TEAM ROCKET!

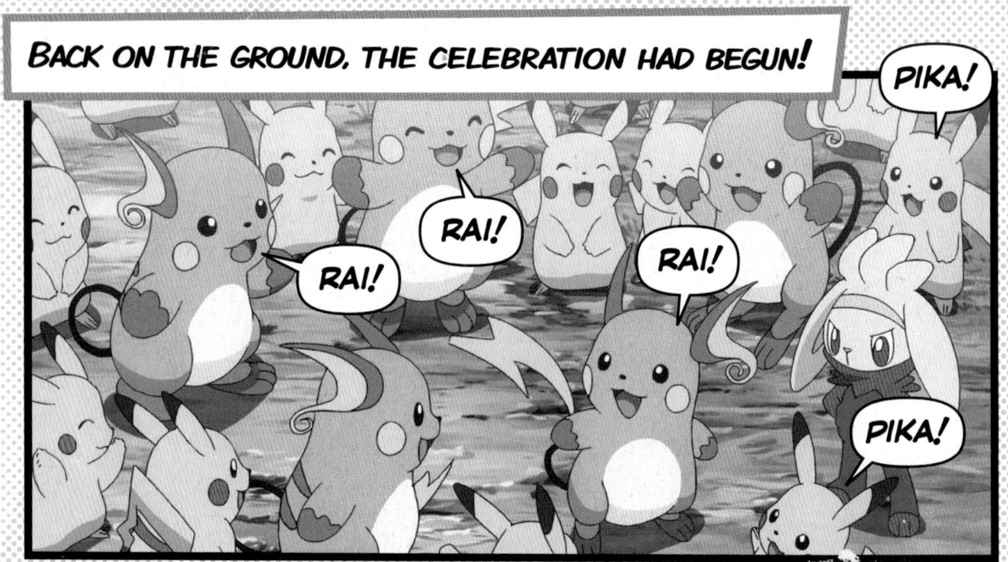
BACK ON THE GROUND, THE CELEBRATION HAD BEGUN!
PIKA!
RAI!
RAI!
RAI!
PIKA!

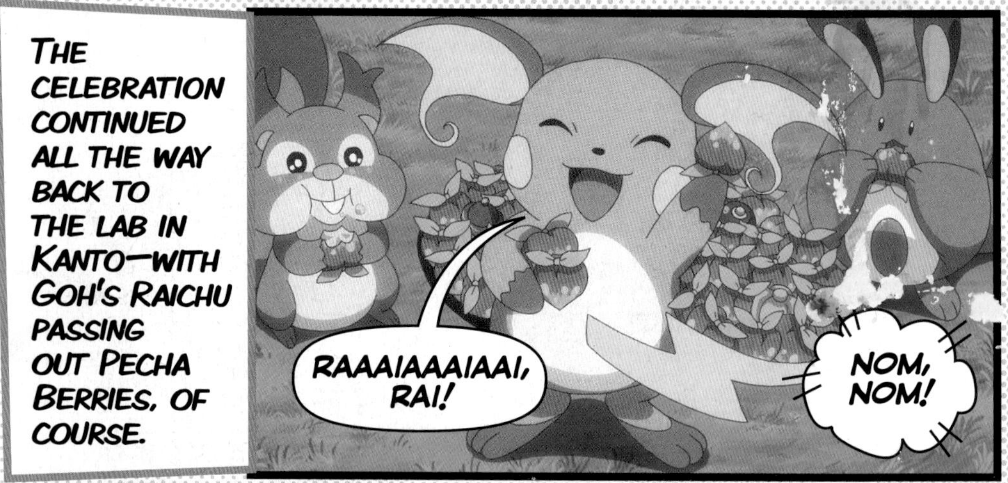
THE CELEBRATION CONTINUED ALL THE WAY BACK TO THE LAB IN KANTO—WITH GOH'S RAICHU PASSING OUT PECHA BERRIES, OF COURSE.
RAAAIAAAIAAI, RAI!
NOM, NOM!

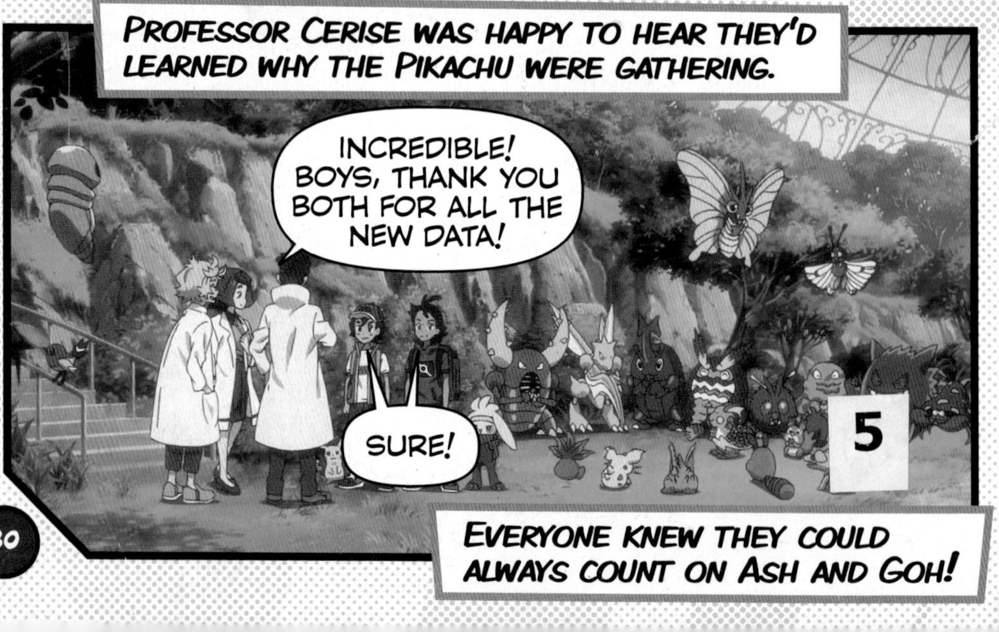
PROFESSOR CERISE WAS HAPPY TO HEAR THEY'D LEARNED WHY THE PIKACHU WERE GATHERING.
INCREDIBLE! BOYS, THANK YOU BOTH FOR ALL THE NEW DATA!
SURE!
5
EVERYONE KNEW THEY COULD ALWAYS COUNT ON ASH AND GOH!